PROFESS

'I, um, ah, fear this is something I had not anticipated,' said Professor Branestawm apologetically. The occasion was when the helpful handbag he had just invented for Mrs Flittersnoop (which *was* handy because it ran on four legs like a dog and you didn't have to carry it) had disgraced itself and her by shoplifting. But the remark would have been equally apt the time the Professor walked into the wrong house in a fog and had to follow Colonel Dedshott's horse home to safety, holding on to its tail, when his self-elevating flower beds got a touch of the unexpected ups and downs and biffed an admirer on the nose. Or when his lovely new fountains at the Town Hall started spouting cocoa.

Poor Professor Branestawm, there's nothing so unpredictable as the invention business. But, to look on the bright side, there's nothing that makes funnier reading either, as you can see from the hilarious histories of the Professor's solar-operated washing line that was programmed to trundle in and out of the house according to rain or shine, or his ingenious but hopelessly unreliable musical housework machine.

Professor Branestawm has been around a long time now, gaining more admirers all the time, and he has gone from strength to strength in this book together with his friends Commander Hardaport, Colonel Dedshott, Miss Frenzie of the Pagwell Publishing Company, and in particular dear Mrs Flittersnoop, so bewildered and so kindly determined to smooth the path of her eccentric employer. There are many more books about him in Puffins.

# NORMAN HUNTER

## *Professor Branestawm round the Bend*

### AND OTHER
### INCREDIBLE ADVENTURES

*With illustrations by*
*Derek Cousins*

## PUFFIN BOOKS

Puffin Books, Penguin Books Ltd, Harmondsworth, Middlesex, England
Penguin Books, 625 Madison Avenue, New York, New York 10022, U.S.A.
Penguin Books Australia Ltd, Ringwood, Victoria, Australia
Penguin Books Canada Ltd, 2801 John Street, Markham, Ontario, Canada L3R 1B4
Penguin Books (N.Z.) Ltd, 182–190 Wairau Road, Auckland 10, New Zealand

—

First published by The Bodley Head Ltd 1977
Published in Puffin Books 1980
Reprinted 1980

—

Copyright © Norman Hunter, 1977
Illustrations © Derek Cousins, 1977
All rights reserved

—

Typeset, printed and bound in Great Britain by
Hazell Watson & Viney Ltd,
Aylesbury, Bucks
Set in Linotype Baskerville

*To my darling wife Binks,*
*partly for being a little bit*
*of Mrs Flittersnoop and a little bit*
*of the Queen of Incrediblania,*
*but mostly for being her*
*own sweet self*

# Contents

# I

## *Professor Branestawm round the Bend*

PROFESSOR BRANESTAWM came carefully down-stairs backwards. This, of course, was the kind of thing the Professor was apt to do, either because he thought he was going upstairs, or because he had his mind on a new invention, or even because he had caught the habit from his next-door neighbour, Commander Hardaport (Retired). Commander Hardaport was an exceedingly naval gentleman, and always came downstairs backwards because sailors have to do that on ships in case of rough seas and because ship's staircases are rather on the vertical side.

But this time was different. The Professor had had a slight accident with an extra truculent invention and had hurt his foot so that he couldn't get down steps unless he did it backwards.

'I am, er, ah, going to Pagwell University this morning,' he said to Mrs Flittersnoop, his house-keeper, who was laying the breakfast table, 'to de-liver a lecture on . . . er, that is to say, I am speaking to them about . . .' He realized he couldn't remember what he was going to lecture about, consulted his notes but found they were diagrams for an invention for special ink that always spelt words correctly, and then discovered he had written the subject of his lecture on a paper serviette. It was one of Mrs Flittersnoop's best, double-thickness, super-strength ones that she kept for visitors but she didn't mind as she felt it was in a good cause.

'Yes, indeed, I'm sure, sir,' she said, deftly moving the Professor's fried egg out of the way before he put his teacup down on it. 'Will you be in to lunch, sir?'

'I, er, yes, of course don't mention it,' said the Professor. He spread marmalade on his fried egg, put salt in his tea, put his hat on the wrong way round and went out.

He arrived at Great Pagwell Station just in time to miss the train before his, which was just as well because he would almost certainly have got on it and it wasn't going anywhere near where he wanted to go.

'Is this my train?' he asked the Station-master, as another train came rattling and zooming in.

'No, it is not,' said the Station-master, deciding to be a bit funny as it was a fine day. 'This train belongs to the Railway Company.'

'Oh, um,' said the Professor. 'Then I am sure they will not mind my using it.'

'Of course, Professor,' said the Station-master. 'Allow me to help you in. Dear, dear, whatever have you done to your foot?'

'An, um, er, slight accident with an invention,' said the Professor. 'That is why I am travelling by train instead of by car, because I find it somewhat, er, difficult to operate the foot levers of the integrating clutch system of my car.'

'Quite, quite,' said the Station-master, giving the Professor a final push into the carriage.

He waved his hands. The passengers waved back thinking what a nice man he was to be so friendly. Something made a buzzing noise somewhere and the train drew out of the station with the Professor sitting tidily in a carriage, on the seat, not up on the rack or in the luggage-van or anywhere else he could easily have been as he was absent-minded.

He started thinking about new inventions. He thought of self-eating rice pudding for people who didn't like it. He pondered over non-sticky glue to keep your fingers clean, and considered the possibility of invisible paint that wouldn't show if you spilt it on the carpet.

And he was so busy thinking of incredible new inventions he only just noticed in time that the train had stopped at a station.

'Er, um, ha, here I am,' he said. He opened the door and began slowly getting out of the carriage backwards because of course with his bad foot he couldn't get out forwards.

But, oh dear, the porters thought he was getting *into* the train and, being nice helpful railway porters, they shouted, 'Hurry along there!' and gave him a helpful push back into the carriage and shut the door.

'I, er, thank you very much but I wish to, er,' he stuttered. But the train was already off to stations new.

It was a good thing for the Professor that that

station was Upper Pagwell, where he didn't have to get out for the University. Because if it had been Pagwell North, where he did have to get out, he would have been carried past his station. On the other hand if he hadn't had a bad foot, which he couldn't have had on either hand if it comes to that, he would have got out at the wrong station as usual and Pagwell University would have been deprived of his lecture.

The Professor sank back on to the seat and went on thinking of disastrous new inventions. He was half-way to thinking of an astounding method for making coal from sawdust and potato peelings when the train pulled into Pagwell North.

'Ha!' said the Professor, coming out of his inventing thoughts. 'This is where I get out.'

He started getting out of the train backwards as before, but again a helpful porter came dashing up to help him. And, of course, once again he thought the Professor was trying to get into the train, not out of it. And once again he helped him back into his carriage.

'But I wish to, er, that is to say, I do not wish, er, um, at least, this is where I . . .' he spluttered.

'That's all right, sir,' shouted the porter. 'You're all right now, sir. Hold tight,' and with a lot of flag-waving and buzzing and hand-signalling the train steamed out of the station, or it would have done if only it had been a steam train and not a diesel electric one.

'Dear me, this is most awkward,' grunted the Pro-

*An astounding method for making coal from sawdust
and potato peelings*

fessor, clashing his spectacles about a bit as the train went zooming off. 'Now I shall have to get out at the next station and catch a bus back. That is to say, if there is a bus. Otherwise I shall have to catch another train back to Pagwell North and that will mean crossing the line by the footbridge, which will, I am afraid, be, um, ah, rather difficult with a bad foot.'

Houses and telegraph poles and people's gardens went streaming past and presently the train slowed down and stopped at Pagwell-by-Poppingford. The Professor started climbing out backwards again of course because it was the only way he could get out.

'Pagwellpoppord!' shouted a porter, which was the railway porters' short way of saying Pagwell-by-Poppingford, only it was so short none of the passengers could understand it except one who used to be a railway porter himself and knew where he was anyway.

But Professor Branestawm didn't care where it was. He only wanted to get out of the train so as to get back to Pagwell North to give his lecture at the University.

'Hurry along there, please!' shouted the porters, and they came running up and helped the Professor most politely back into his carriage, thinking, as the other porters had done, that he was trying to get in. And off went the train again carrying the Professor farther and farther from where he wanted to be.

'Tut, tut, I shall never get there in time to give my lecture,' gasped the Professor. He pulled the alarm chain without bothering how much it was going to cost, but it came off in his hand. He leaned out of the window even though there were severe notices saying he mustn't.

On went the train. *Errk!* it snorted through tunnels. *Zimzimetty zim*, it rattled across switches. *Rm-m-m*, it zoomed over bridges. Other people's houses and other people's gardens and other people's dogs and cats and flowers and vegetables shot past at high speed. People who had no lectures to give at Universities were overtaken and left behind.

Pagwell Muffington came and went. The train stopped at Pretty Pagwell, Pagwell-on-the-Hill and Pagwell Road. But each time the Professor tried to get out the porters thought he was getting in, because he tried to get out backwards. And each time they helped him back and the train went on.

'Oh dear, I shall never get anywhere like this,' groaned the Professor. 'I shall never be able to get out of this train. I shall starve to death. Oh, oh, oh!'

At Pagwell University they were looking at their watches, gazing at the clocks and checking the time with the invisible lady on the telephone.

'What can have happened to Professor Branestawm?' they said. But they knew so many things could have happened to the Professor and probably had, it wasn't much use guessing.

'Ring up his home,' said the Dean, 'and find out if

he's been delayed or forgotten about the lecture or got himself immersed in an invention.'

Mrs Flittersnoop said oh yes indeed, the Professor had left in good time. But after the University man had rung off she was a bit worried and so she called Colonel Dedshott of the Catapult Cavaliers. He was the Professor's extra special friend, always ready to have his head made to go round and round listening to the Professor explaining an invention, or to go dashing off in several directions to rescue the Professor from dangers or help him out of fixes. He got his Catapult Cavaliers out to see if they could find where the Professor had gone. They started by inquiring at all the railway stations, with photos of the Professor, to find out if anyone like him had got on the train. And at the very first station they asked, Great Pagwell, the Station-master and porters said, oh yes, definitely, the Professor had got on at Great Pagwell.

But, oh goodness, the porter at Pagwell North said he had got on there too. And at Pagwell-by-Poppingford they said he had got on there. And the same at Pagwell Muffington, Pretty Pagwell, Pagwell-on-the-Hill and Pagwell Road.

'Ha, nonsense, by Jove!' grunted Colonel Dedshott. 'Professor's a clever chap, of course, but can't have got on a train at *all* these stations. My word, perhaps some villains are impersonating him.' But as the Colonel couldn't think of even an unlikely reason why anyone should want to impersonate the Professor that didn't help.

'Do you think perhaps the Professor has invented a thing that has accidentally split him into a dozen Professors?' inquired Mrs Flittersnoop, hoping very much it was impossible, but you had to consider everything, hadn't you?

Soon word came in from Pagwell Woods, Pagwell Green and Pagwell Junction that the Professor had been seen getting on a train at all these stations. But, of course, what he had really been seen doing was trying to get *off* the train. Everybody thought he was trying to get on and helped him in.

'If only someone else would get in this carriage,' groaned the Professor. 'Then I could tell them I wanted to get out.'

But nobody did get in because it was one of those slow trains that stop at every possible station and in between as well if it can, and so nobody got on it unless they only wanted to go to the next station, and none of them got in the Professor's carriage because he was always in the way trying to get out. And anyway, thought the Professor, what was the use at this stage? If he had managed to get out of the train at some far-off place like Pagwell Woods he would have got in such a muddle trying to get back to Pagwell North he might have been worse off than he was now, where at least he was under cover if it rained.

The Catapult Cavaliers continued diligently showing photos of the Professor all round to see if he had been seen anywhere and kept finding he had been seen getting on a train at nearly every station the railway had in stock.

Meanwhile the Dean of Pagwell University was getting annoyed. 'Here I have all the students assembled, that is to say all except those who couldn't come because of illness or wouldn't come because they didn't care for lectures or haven't come because of some other reason, and no Professor Branestawm and therefore no lecture.'

'That sounds quite logical to me,' said the Assistant Dean, shaking biscuit crumbs out of his gown because he had just had his coffee break. 'And perhaps less embarrassing for us than if Professor Branestawm had arrived and no students had turned up to listen to his lecture.'

'Pah!' snorted the Dean, which is a rather un-University thing to snort. 'We shall have to think up something for the students to do now they're here.'

'How about party games?' suggested the Assistant Dean.

'Party games!' screeched the Dean, cramming his mortar board down over his ears. 'Party games at a University? Whoever heard of such a thing?'

'Well, I did just now,' said the Assistant Dean, 'when I mentioned it, and again when you objected to it.'

'*Pah*, all over again!' cried the Dean. 'You go and lecture to the students to keep them quiet while I ring the Professor's house again.'

So the Assistant Dean went off and lectured to the students, which didn't keep them quiet at all because they were disappointed at not hearing a lecture from Professor Branestawm.

The train with Professor Branestawm still unwill-ingly in it went rattling on. It stopped at Pagwell Halt, at Pagwell Halfpenny, Pagwell Hill and Pag-well Bridge. And the Professor didn't manage to get out at any of them, partly because the porters at each station thought he was trying to get in and partly because he had almost given up hope of ever getting out of that train.

Presently the train stopped at another station.

'It seems hardly worthwhile trying to get out,' moaned the Professor. Then he said, 'Good gracious, how very strange! This station seems familiar. Surely I, um, recognize that machine that sells you sausage-flavoured crisps if you put the right coin in the right slot and the machine isn't empty. And I, er, believe I recognize that sign saying *Lost Property*. I've always wondered how it could be lost if they knew where it was. Dear me, can I have been here before?'

Yes, he could have and he had. For, strange sur-prise, the train had arrived back at Great Pagwell station! That part of the line went round the vari-ous Pagwells in a railway circle and came back to where it started.

'Well,' groaned the Professor, when he finally realized where he was, 'I've heard of people going round the bend, but this is really going too far round it. If I don't manage to get out here I'm imprisoned for life in a train. Wonderful headline for the papers but most, um, ah, inconvenient for me.'

But it was all right. The Station-master at Great

Pagwell of course knew about the Professor's bad foot and helped him to get out of the train. Then he charged him the fare from Pagwell North right round the outer circle and back to Great Pagwell, which seems a bit unfair but railways are very strict about passengers travelling without paying, even if they don't particularly want to travel.

The telephone was ringing as Professor Branestawm crept wearily into his house. It was the Dean of Pagwell University who had just managed to get on to the Professor's house again after getting connected to the Fire Station, the Dairy and the Home for Lost Squirrels by mistake.

'Ah, Professor!' cried the Dean. 'We were expecting you at the University to give your lecture.'

'Um, ah, yes,' said the Professor, and he explained what had happened, which made the Dean's head go round and round nearly as fast as Colonel Dedshott's did at the Professor's explanations, but not nearly as fast as the train had gone round with the Professor shut up in it.

'I think it would be better,' said the Dean, 'if we brought the students to you to save you coming here with your bad foot.'

'Er, um, ah yes, quite so,' said the Professor, not seeing how he could get to the University *without* his bad foot as he was rather attached to it.

So the students from Pagwell University crammed into the Professor's sitting-room with some standing in corners and some sitting on the bookshelves, which seemed a suitable place for students to sit.

And Mrs Flittersnoop came up with tea and home-made scones all round.

And Professor Branestawm was at last able to give his notable lecture on the efficient and economical way to use the railway.

## 2

## *The Wild Washing-Day*

'THERE now,' cried Mrs Flittersnoop in alarm, 'if it hasn't started to rain! I must get the washing in.'

'If it hasn't started to rain,' put in the Professor in his most helpful voice, 'you need not get the washing in until it does start.'

But Mrs Flittersnoop was already buried under sheets and pillowcases and pyjamas while the rain pattered happily down, making pretty noises which Mrs Flittersnoop was not prepared to appreciate.

'Um, ah, let me help,' cried the Professor, dashing forward gallantly and treading on the end of a sheet Mrs Flittersnoop was rather wrapped up in, which caused her to fall over and trip up the Professor. By the time they had got themselves sorted out and the washing safely indoors two things had happened. It had stopped raining and the washing was covered in muddy footmarks.

'I shall have to wash them again, that's all,' she cried, turning on the hot tap and getting out her extra large size, bargain offer packet of Miracle Washing Powder that Gets Whites Whiter than White with 3p off recommended price.

Meanwhile, the sun had come out and it was a lovely day for drying the clothes Mrs Flittersnoop had just re-washed.

'Allow me to give you a hand with hanging them out,' said the Professor, when Mrs Flittersnoop emerged from the steam with the last washed sock.

There was a great deal of 'Be careful with my best blouse!' and 'Have you any more, um, ah, clothes pegs?' and 'Don't let that pillowcase drop on the grass!' and other washing conversation. The Professor managed to peg the shirt he was wearing on the line by mistake and Mrs Flittersnoop only just got him unpegged in time to prevent him from being hauled up with the rest of the washing.

'There now,' she said, when the last towel and final piece of teacloth was pegged out and the line hauled up. 'They'll soon be dry with this sun.'

But the very next moment some rain clouds blew up, down came a considerable amount of rain and they had to gather all the washing in again.

And by the time they had it safely inside the house, which took some doing as the Professor got himself entangled in a tablecloth, the sun had come out again and they had to hang the washing out once more.

Over at Pagwell Vicarage there was a similar problem. Maisie and Daisie, the Vicar's twin daughters, were having a nice sunbathe in their new bikinis, both exactly alike, when the rain came down on them and they had to dash indoors before their false eyelashes started dissolving.

But they had no sooner got inside and started to put on some clothes when out came the sun and they had to strip off and rush out again.

Then before they could get toasted even a pale biscuit colour the rain came down and drove them in.

'It, ah, really seems to me,' gasped Professor Branestawm, after five more ins and outs with the washing, 'that we are managing to get the washing out when it is raining and inside when the sun is shining.'

'Yes, indeed, I'm sure, sir,' said Mrs Flittersnoop, who was wondering whether it wouldn't be quicker and easier to put the whole lot in the oven and bake them dry, but unfortunately she had a rather fierce fruit cake cooking and daren't open the oven door in case it went flop.

Professor Branestawm too was having a good think, which would probably turn out to be a bad think because it would almost certainly lead to a disastrously ingenious invention.

'The sun is now being used to warm people's houses,' he said to himself. 'Now if I can devise a way of using solar rays to operate an automatic, er, washing-line, it should be possible so to arrange, um, matters that the washing will be out in the garden when it is sunny and safely inside the house if it rains, instead of the other way about as we have been experiencing.'

Colonel Dedshott, who had just dropped in for a cup of tea, thought it was a jolly good idea, though he himself never bothered whether it was raining or not. His Catapult Cavalier soldiers were quite used to getting soaking wet or boiling hot, and being in full marching order, piled up with everything but a colour television set and an aspidistra with the scorching sun beating down on them, or running about in little short pants and no vest, doing exercises, in an ice-cold, north-easterly wind. A soldier's life is very trying, but at least they always know they're going to get their pocket-money.

'There is already a method of heating houses by solar radiation,' said the Professor. 'All you have to do is take the roof off and replace it with solar panels. And if you can do that, why shouldn't I use the same principle to move the washing out into the garden while it is sunny?'

'Hum, ha, yes, by Jove!' grunted the Colonel, who didn't think there could be a military answer to that.

Just then the Vicar arrived, with his wife, to consult Mrs Flittersnoop about lemonade for the vicarage garden party, and the Professor started to tell the Vicar about his solar radiation-operated washing-line.

'Well, I suppose it would be all right,' murmured the Vicar, who felt that he ought to feel it was a bit unchristian harnessing the sun to warm houses, but then you had to have progress, didn't you?

'I think it's a positively marvellous idea!' said the Vicar's wife, having got the lemonade organized with Mrs Flittersnoop. 'I'm always having to rush out and get the washing in because it comes on to rain. My husband, of course, prays for a fine washing-day but we don't always get the right answer.'

So the Professor disappeared into his inventory and began the task of inventing an invention that would make sure the washing was in the garden when the sun was out and inside the house when it wasn't. And meanwhile Maisie and Daisie solved their problem by buying themselves a jar of some cream with a very expensive smell that was highly recommended by the advertisements for giving ladies a lovely sun tan without having to go out in the sun at all. Unfortunately it brought Maisie and Daisie out in spots and they had to go and buy more jars of special ointment for hiding spots.

Professor Branestawm's world-shaking invention for keeping the washing in the sun took him a bit of time because he kept getting his molecules mixed up with his atoms, and at first his attempts at controlling solar radiation for drying clothes only made his tea get cold because he forgot to drink it. But at last the first sun-operated automatic washing-line in the world was ready to astonish the neighbours.

'Queer-looking craft,' said Commander Hardaport (Retired). 'Never seen a rig like it in me life.'

'Ah, that is because you are looking at the bare framework,' said the Professor. 'When it is covered with washing you will find it more, ah, recognizable.'

Mrs Flittersnoop brought out the week's wash and, in spite of the Professor giving her a helping hand, she actually managed to get it all arranged on the arms and lines of the machine, where it looked rather like something left over from the Spanish Armada.

The Vicar's wife, who had brought her washing along to have it done, sort of for charity while the demonstration was on, arranged the Vicar's pyjamas and surplices tastefully alongside the vicarage table-cloths. By this time the Professor's special washing-line had all sails set and was straining at its moorings.

'Ha!' exclaimed the Commander, a nautical gleam flickering in his eyes. 'Got your mizzen tops'ls under your t'gallants, I see, and your spinnakers are abaft your royals. Most unseamanlike. Never make a passage like that, y'know.'

But the Professor's sun-operated washing line wasn't going to be put off course by naval talk from a next-door neighbour. As the sun came out it emitted a whirring sound like a cuckoo clock going back-wards. Mrs Flittersnoop's best nightdress spread out, tablecloths flapped and the whole thing went glid-ing into the garden, sweeping Colonel Dedshott into a wheelbarrow and finally coming to rest on the calceolaria bed.

'Well, indeed I'm sure, I never, sir,' exclaimed Mrs Flittersnoop.

'The, er, washing will now remain out in the gar-den as long as the sun shines,' explained the Profes-sor. 'But if it should come on to rain my invention will bring it all safely indoors out of the wet.'

'Pity we can't make it rain so as to see it do it,' said the Commander.

*It looked rather like something left over from the*
*Spanish Armada*

'Can't you make it rain for us, Professor?' asked Mr Stinckz-Bernagh, the science master from Pagwell College who had come to see what scientifically controlled laundry looked like. 'You did it once with a weather machine, I remember.'

But the Professor wasn't going to muck about with the weather any more. He had had enough of mauve snow mixed up with heat waves.

Just then Mr Marmaduke Mushington Mobley, who lived next door to the Professor on the other side from Commander Hardaport, turned on the hose to water his garden and a spray or two fell on the washing. Instantly the sun-operated clothes-line went about and tacked briskly back into the house, which would have taken the wind right out of Commander Hardaport's sails if he had had them with him.

'Goodness me, indeed, sir!' cried Mrs Flittersnoop, just getting out of the way before the washing-line could clap her best nightdress on her, which she thought would have been rather indelicate with so many gentlemen present.

Mr Marmaduke Mushington Mobley next door had got his hose under control now and was spraying his moon daisies, and so the washing-line went sailing out again into the sun under full canvas and hove to beside the sweet peas. But when Mr Marmaduke Mushington Mobley finished spraying his moon daisies and rushed across the garden to water his roses, another shower of water accidentally fell on the washing. The Professor's machine conscientiously sailed back indoors and promptly sailed out again.

Then what must happen but some real, genuine, wet rain came splashing down and the Professor's wonderful washing-line put its helm over and shot back inside the house, where it sailed into the dining-room and moored alongside the sideboard.

'Stop it! Stop it!' cried Mrs Flittersnoop. 'I've only just cleaned the silver.'

But the machine wasn't interested in silver, whether just cleaned or not. It disembarked most of the washing all over the room. The top of the Vicar's pyjamas was seated at the dining-table along with the Professor's shirts and Mrs Flittersnoop's best drip-dry blouses, where they seemed to be waiting for tea to be served.

'I, er, fear these sudden changes in the, um, ah, apparent weather have disturbed the rather delicate balance of the solar panel control units,' cried the Professor. He tried to get the washing back on the machine but the Vicar's pyjamas obviously weren't going to get up from the table till they had had their tea.

' 'Vast heaving!' cried Commander Hardaport (Retired), waving a telescope at the machine, which took it away from him, pegged it on one of its lines and shot out into the garden again as the sun had come out.

Meantime Maisie and Daisie had tried another kind of sun-tan cream but this turned them pale green and made them look as if they were made of marzipan.

'Let's go and ask Professor Branestawm to invent something to give us a nice tan while we stay indoors and play records,' said either Maisie or Daisie.

'Great!' cried Daisie or Maisie.

They arrived at the Professor's just in time to be scooped up by the washing-line and pegged out alongside the rock garden.

'Oh my goodness, my daughters!' wailed the Vicar's wife, while the Vicar sent up a hurried barrage of hopeful prayers and rushed to the rescue, accompanied by Colonel Dedshott and Commander Hardaport, uttering military and naval exclamations.

'Help!' cried Maisie and Daisie, both in the same kind of voice.

The machine dodged the rescuers and beat hurriedly to port among the gooseberry bushes.

'*Ow!*' cried Maisie (or was it Daisie?). 'I've heard that old story about being found under a gooseberry bush but I don't want to be sent back there.'

Colonel Dedshott took a swipe at the machine with his sword and cut the tops off two gooseberry bushes and the legs off the Vicar's pyjamas.

The machine gybed, went about and shot round to the front of the house, down the garden path and out into the road just as a van from the Great Pagwell Laundry came along.

*Bong! Crash! Wallop, bing, tinkle, tinkle!* The laundry van hit the washing-line machine amidships. The air was full of accident noises and laundry sounds. The Professor, Colonel Dedshott and the Vicar came tearing up yelling advice and warnings.

But the Laundry Man was a very dedicated washing collector. He was out to collect washing and here was washing that needed collecting, so he bundled it all into his van and drove off. His van was a plentifully robust one and had hardly suffered at all in the crash except for some of the painted letters being scraped off, so that the name on the van read *Great Pagwell La dry*, which made it sound a rather French sort of laundry.

But the Professor's incredible, mechanical, sun-operated washing-line had had it, three times over. Nothing was left but an awful lot of clothes-line and a great many bits of assorted metal.

'Oh, the washing!' cried Mrs Flittersnoop.

'My husband's pyjamas!' moaned the Vicar's wife.

But it was all right because the Great Pagwell Laundry were frightfully efficient and managed to return nearly all the washing to its rightful owners, carefully re-washed and dried indoors out of the rain. Only one pair of the Vicar's pyjamas went astray and that landed at an Oxfam shop.

And Mrs Flittersnoop felt just a little bit relieved that she could now hang the washing out on a nice simple, innocent, inoffensive washing-line that wouldn't answer back. But being a very careful lady, she now hung it out to dry indoors to be on the safe side. Unless of course, the weather forecast said it was going to rain, and then she hung it out in the garden knowing they were due for a fine, sunny day.

# 3

## *The Professor Deals with Inflation*

*Squeak, squeak, squeak, puff, puff, squeak.*

Was it mice nibbling at the foundations of the Town Hall? Could it be a new invention of Professor Branestawm's that needed oiling? No, it was the Vicar of Great Pagwell pumping up his bicycle tyres ready to visit deserving people.

'Ha, Vicar!' cried Commander Hardaport (Retired), rolling up with a telescope under one arm and the *Yachting World* under the other. 'Getting inflation under control, I see, ha ha ha!'

'Dear me, I wish I could,' murmured the Vicar, putting his pump back on his bicycle upside down. 'Things are getting serious, you know, Commander, most serious.' He said it twice because he felt it sounded more serious that way. 'Everything is costing so much.'

'Ha, yes,' grunted the Commander, opening his telescope and looking at a little bird on a tree, which resented it and flew away. 'The rates are too high for a start. Shan't pay 'em. And then there are the dustmen coming only once a fortnight. Don't know what to do with all the rubbish. Better give it to the *Pagwell Gazette* – they can print it with the other stuff.'

'I think we should form a deputation and see the

Council about it,' said the Vicar, wishing he could charge for seats in church to get money to have the organ seen to.

'My word, yes,' shouted the Commander. 'Get Colonel Dedshott along, and Professor Branestawm. Make 'em listen, by jingo! Clear decks for action.'

Colonel Dedshott was only too ready for action, whether any decks were cleared for it or not. And as for Professor Branestawm, he immediately had fifteen ideas for beating inflation, some of which would have abolished rates, some of which would have abolished the Council and some of which could easily have abolished Pagwell itself.

Meantime Pagwell Council were already having an emergency meeting on very economy lines to decide what to do about inflation and high prices. They held it in the basement instead of in the Council Chamber because it felt more economical. All the Councillors wore old clothes so as to look as if they weren't spending any money and they had their morning tea half an hour late with not enough sugar in it.

'Hrmp!' said the Mayor. 'I think we should start with economies in the Council. It will set a good example, you know.'

'Hear, hear!' cried the Councillors, who were all for setting good examples as long as they didn't have to follow them.

'I suggest that in future the Council's proceedings are recorded on the backs of old envelopes instead of in that expensive leather-bound book,' said the Mayor.

'And don't let's call them minutes,' said the Drains Councillor. 'Make it seconds, that's a lot less.'

'No, no, no!' cried the Treasurer. 'What we want is not so much ways of *saving* money as ways of getting more.'

'We can't put the rates up any higher,' protested the Parks and Gardens Councillor, who had already got into trouble for not paying his.

All these plans for beating inflation had progressed on a friendly basis for some time. Nobody had called anybody a rude name. Nobody had thrown anything and hardly anybody had shouted much above a whisper. But inflation was continuing all over the place and the Council decided to do something really drastic.

'We must reduce spending however much it costs,' cried the Town Clerk. 'And we must make more money however much we lose. I suggest we call in Professor Branestawm to help.'

But Professor Branestawm didn't need any calling in. He was already stamping round the Town Hall accompanied by the Vicar, Colonel Dedshott and Commander Hardaport (Retired) and an excitable door-keeper man who was trying to tell them they weren't allowed in. Eventually they tracked down the Councillors, and the meeting blew up in table-thumpings and teeth-gnashings and highly inflammable language as the Professor and his friends told the Council what to do about things.

'I, er, um, ah,' said Professor Branestawm, after Commander Hardaport (Retired) had at last blown a fog horn he had brought with him to get some quiet. 'That is to say, what we need is some device which will make people want to pay money to the Council. Something that will cause them to, um, ah, rush along with money only too anxious to pay it.'

'Ha, ha, ha! He, he, he! Ho, ho, ho!' laughed the Councillors, who thought that was a better joke than the ones on the telly.

'If we could do that we needn't have any rates,' said the Treasurer, shivering slightly at the thought of not having rates and having to do without those lovely final demand notices printed in red to look more alarming.

'Precisely!' said the Professor. 'It will make Pagwell the happiest town in the world.'

'What will?' asked the Drains Councillor, who had been asleep and had missed everything.

'Something to make the people come rushing here, gladly giving us money,' said the Mayor.

The Drains Councillor got so excited at hearing this that he nearly choked himself and somebody sent for a plumber to clear him.

'Nonsense!' roared the Councillor in charge of libraries, who was cross because his allowance for buying comics had been cut. 'The thing's impossible! Nobody likes paying money to the Council. How are you going to get them to come rushing along to do it and like it?'

'Fun fair!' said Professor Branestawm, waving his five pairs of spectacles about. 'Dodgem cars, roundabouts, big dippers, haunted houses, water chutes . . .'

'Accompanied by military bands, by Jove!' put in Colonel Dedshott, who was determined that the Catapult Cavaliers should play their part.

'And miniature gunboats on the canal!' cried Commander Hardaport (Retired), banging the table with his telescope and upsetting the Mayor's tea. 'Naval displays! Sinking the submarine – sort of nautical coconut shy, ha ha!'

The Councillors opened their mouths and didn't say anything. They were speechless for the first time in living memory. They gave wonderful imitations of surprised goldfish. They flapped their hands like astonished seals. But at last they recovered long enough to instruct Professor Branestawm to proceed with all speed to create the Great Pagwell Fun Fair to cause people to come hurrying up with handfuls of lovely money, and then the meeting broke up without any confusion, except that all the Councillors' heads were going round and round even faster than Colonel Dedshott's.

Professor Branestawm's inventory buzzed and whizzed and hummed with activity. Coloured smoke and fancy stars emerged, and slight bangs exploded now and then. Mrs Flittersnoop got tired of trying to push cups of tea and sandwiches through the windows and asked the Meals-on-Wheels people to deal with the Professor. But their dinners were only run over by some of his inventions, which turned them into wheels-on-meals.

Round about the time that the second final notices

for paying the rates were due to go out, the Great Pagwell Municipal Fun Fair went into business. There was no opening ceremony in case people thought it was extravagant. The Mayor stayed at home, put on his robes and said, 'I declare the Fun Fair open', to himself.

'Cool!' exclaimed the Great Pagwellians, when they saw the Fair, and rushed in with money at the ready, just as the Professor had said they would.

First of all, there were dodgem cars, specially contrived so that they went out of the Fun Fair and swept the streets. That not only saved Pagwell Council the cost of having the streets swept but also brought in money from the people who paid to go in the cars.

'Of course people have to pay for having the streets swept,' said the Town Clerk. 'Only they prefer to pay for it by dodgem car rides and do it themselves, so everybody's happy.'

And happiest of all were the street-sweeping men who took over mowing the grass in the Pagwell Parks so that the mowing men could be released for other duties, and most of *them* were so old they preferred to stay at home and mow their own lawns.

Then there was an ingenious roundabout that worked the pumping station for the Pagwell water supply. That saved no end of money because the pumping-station men were then free to join the police, and criminals began to be caught three times as often, which was still hardly at all.

'Good old Branestawm, my word, what!' ex-

*Dodgem cars, specially contrived so that they went out of the Fun Fair and swept the streets*

claimed Colonel Dedshott. He made a bonfire of all his rate demands and got fined half as much as the rates he didn't pay for emitting smoke in a smoke-less zone.

The Fun Fair also included an ingenious game called 'Mending a hole in the road'. For this you paid your money and were given a little cart full of road-mending equipment and a map showing where all the holes were. You simply picked your hole, dashed off and filled it and came back. And if you filled your hole more quickly than anyone else had done you got your money back. But of course only one person could get his money back on that rule, so Pagwell Council made almost enough money to fill the holes in their budget.

Another Branestawm Fun Fair device was the 'Traffic Warden Game'. In this you paid for a war-den's hat and a book of tickets, and then you went around the streets sticking tickets on all the cars that shouldn't be there. You got commission on the fines the owners had to pay, so that you made a nice profit. But some enthusiastic players stuck tickets on their own cars in the excitement and got fined more than they made. And one frightful player stuck a ticket on the car of the Head Policeman and was nearly sent to prison for a thousand years.

All these ingenious devices of Professor Brane-stawm's drew such a crowd and collected so much money that Pagwell Council were able not only to abolish rates altogether but actually to pay out pocket-money bonuses to the residents.

Nothing could possibly be more delightful. Pagwell became the most envied place in the country. Would-be emigrants from other places formed long snaky queues, hoping to find somewhere to live in Pagwell. Some people were willing even to move in to dog kennels but the dogs refused to move out.

'Marvellous, dear chap,' cried Commander Hardaport, slapping the Professor on the back.

'Most satisfactory,' purred the Vicar, who had been given a lovely lump of money by Pagwell Council to buy a new organ for the church.

'Yes, indeed, I'm sure, sir,' agreed Mrs Flittersnoop.

But a week later things began to happen.

The people who took out the dodgem cars found the streets were now so clean that there was nothing to sweep, and so they used the cars instead to go shopping. Then the Fun Fair traffic wardens gleefully swooped down and clapped tickets on them. But there was some argument as to whether a dodgem car was a ticketable vehicle within the meaning of the Act, and anyway the owners of the cars were Pagwell Council and they had to pay the fines themselves. The roundabouts were so busy and flew round at such a speed that water was pumped far too energetically and Pagwell householders got a bathful squirted over them every time they turned on a tap.

Then the mend-a-hole-in-the-road game made the roads so smooth and pleasant that traffic that didn't want to go anywhere near Pagwell went that way because it was such a beautiful ride. And the Pagwellians couldn't get out of their houses for the traffic congestion that was caused.

'This is terrible!' gasped the Town Clerk. 'Professor, you *must* do something about it. Your inventions! Your ideas! They have gone wrong as usual. Most inconvenient. Pagwell is in chaos.'

'Um, ah, pardon me,' said Professor Branestawm, arranging his spectacles firmly and going all indignant. 'My inventions have *not* gone wrong, they are working perfectly. It is your citizens who have gone wrong. If they choose to use my inventions in a way I did not intend that is not my, er, um, fault.' And he stalked away in a middle-sized dudgeon.

Things got worse. Professor Branestawm's ingenious ideas were working splendidly. But the Pagwellians were even more ingenious in using them in all sorts of unexpected ways. People had themselves a ball. They got up to larks. They enjoyed themselves far too much. And poor old Pagwell Council was in a terrible state.

'Inflation will overtake us again!' moaned the Mayor.

'We shall have to charge rates again!' cried the Town Clerk.

It was no use calling in Colonel Dedshott and the Catapult Cavaliers this time. Attacking the dodgem cars or setting about roundabouts or charging the traffic wardens wouldn't help at all.

Professor Branestawm waved his hands and his spectacles flew about.

'Can't you invent a machine for putting things back as they were?' groaned the Mayor.

Professor Branestawm couldn't. But what he could do was invent a rival Fun Fair with much more exciting things in it, to lure away the Pagwellians from the road-sweeping dodgem cars, the hole-mending, the traffic warden game and the water-pumping roundabouts.

And that is what he did.

But it took Great Pagwell simply ages to get back to having the roads swept and mended by road-sweeping and mending men, and having proper traffic wardens putting tickets on cars, and letting the pumping station do without its roundabouts. And some of the people who used to do those jobs didn't want to came back so that the Catapult Cavaliers had to be pressed into service temporarily, and students had to do the jobs in their holidays. But at last Great Pagwell was itself again, with nice expensive rates and inflation doing its thing once more.

And Professor Branestawm had the great satisfaction of knowing that for once it wasn't his inventions that went wrong but the people who used them. It was a lovely change.

# 4

## Supermarket Afloat

PROFESSOR BRANESTAWM was in the Miracle
Marvel Supermarket in Great Pagwell. And he was
there on purpose too. He hadn't got there by mistake instead of Pagwell University. He wasn't there
instead of giving a lecture in the Town Hall and he
hadn't arrived there through missing the way home.
He had actually gone there deliberately. It was to do
some shopping for Mrs Flittersnoop, to leave her
free to get the washing done, pop down to sister
Aggie's to see how little Esme's spots were doing and
to darn those of the Professor's socks he hadn't invented into machines or used as paint rags. And, of
course, to make a nice change for her.

'Um, ah,' muttered the Professor, gazing at rows
and rows of packets and bottles and jars and boxes,
all screaming at him that they saved him 2p or
offered him a free holiday in Spanish Morocco or
the chance to win a twenty-cylinder souped-up
sports car with nine wheels and ten speeds.

He was trying to remember what it was Mrs Flittersnoop had asked him to get, because the shopping
list she had given him had blown away outside the
butcher's.

'I must, er, apply logic to this matter,' he muttered. 'Now what does a woman always want in the way of shopping?' He found he had no idea. Then he thought, 'Mrs Flittersnoop is almost certain to want what other ladies want from a supermarket. So I shall just follow some other lady round and buy what she buys.'

This worked all right until the lady he was following bought five coconuts and eight loaves of bread for her birds and ducks, ten tins of dog-food for her cats, who were rather fierce cats and thought cat-food was a bit cissy, and fifteen packets of iced biscuits with funny faces on them, as she was going to give a children's party. Fortunately, before the Professor could buy all these things, which could have put Mrs Flittersnoop in several tizzies, the lady complained to the manager that a man was following her about.

'Now then, sir,' said the manager, coming up to the Professor, but the lady stopped him.

'Dear me!' she said. 'Why surely it's Professor Branestawm, isn't it?' She peered at him through her own spectacles which hung round her neck on a sort of dog lead so that she wouldn't lose them. 'Why, my dear Professor, how fortunate to meet you! You are just the man we need.'

'Er, um, yes, I suppose,' muttered the Professor.

'My name is Trumpington-Smawl,' said the lady. 'I live in one of those bungalows in River Lane, you know, and it is so awkward about the groceries.'

'Er, um, ah, of course,' said the Professor, feeling as if his head was going to start going round and round, as Colonel Dedshott's did when he listened to the Professor's explanations.

'They won't deliver,' went on Mrs Trumpington-Smawl. 'These supermarkets, you know. They won't deliver the groceries as they used to do in the old days. Most unjust I call it, especially with the price we pay for things these days. So we have to carry everything home.'

'Er, yes, that would be the logical solution,' said the Professor, his brains beginning to hum a bit.

'But it is extremely awkward,' went on Mrs Trumpington-Smawl, putting down her wire basket on the Professor's foot. 'You see, we live on the other side of the river, and to get to the shops we have to come all the way up River Lane and across Pagwell Bridge and down the other side. But we can't go down the other side because that is a one-way street coming up. So we have to drive all round the town in order to come up the one-way street.'

'Hum,' said the Professor, thinking hard about decimalization so as to stop his head from going round.

'Then, to get home again we have to cross the river by the bridge and go down River Lane. But we can't go *down* River Lane because River Lane is a one-way street coming *up*, and so we have to go right out into the country in order to come up River Lane to our bungalows.'

'Yes, yes,' said the Professor. 'But how can I be of help to you? I cannot, I am afraid, persuade the supermarket to deliver your groceries, unless . . .' He pulled all his pairs of spectacles off and stuffed them

in his pocket. 'Unless . . .' he said. 'Good gracious,
how clever of me! Why, yes, of course, Mrs Bugler-
Large,' he cried, clapping the lady on the back so
that *her* spectacles fell off and swung to and fro on
their chain. 'Leave it to me. I fancy I have your
problems already solved.' He raised his hat and a
packet of brown sugar he had put there to save carrying it, fell out and burst all over Mrs Trumpington-
Smawl's cats' dog-food. Then he rushed home with
practically nothing Mrs Flittersnoop wanted and
several things she didn't want.

'You haven't got it, sir,' she said, rummaging
through the things the Professor had bought.

'I haven't got what?' asked the Professor, still
thinking about Mrs Trumpington-Smawl and her
grocery delivery.

'Fadeless blancmange powder,' said Mrs Flittersnoop. 'The last blancmange I made, a lovely bright
pink it was, turned white in the night.'

Sister Aggie had said it couldn't have been fright-
ened by anything because Mrs Flittersnoop was
noted for her exceedingly courageous blancmanges
which never even wobbled no matter how much you
shook them.

'I shall bring the supermarket to their doors,' said
the Professor.

'To whose doors, sir?' asked Mrs Flittersnoop.

'Those people who live in bungalows in River
Lane,' said the Professor. And he explained to Mrs
Flittersnoop what Mrs Trumpington-Smawl had ex-
plained to him.

'Yes, indeed, I'm sure, sir,' said Mrs Flittersnoop,

and she stopped thinking about nervous blancmanges and went upstairs to get on with the bedrooms, because she could see some rather violent inventing was about to take place and she preferred
not to be there.

'A supermarket afloat!' cried Professor Branestawm. 'A sort of QE3, loaded with groceries and
cruising round to serve the bungalow dwellers in
River Lane.'

'Marvellous, my word, jolly good!' cried Commander Hardaport (Retired), dancing a hornpipe.
'In keeping with our great maritime traditions, you
know. Rule Britannia, and remember to keep to the
starboard bank!'

'Ha, by Jove, yes!' agreed Colonel Dedshott, who
had joined the Professor in Commander Hardaport's little cabin-study with its round windows and
fancy binnacles. 'Pity it couldn't be done by military
manoeuvres, but see the point, hrrm.'

'The supermarket won't deliver because the customers can be persuaded to take their groceries
home,' said the Professor. 'But if we organize a
supermarket on a launch and cruise round serving
the bungalow dwellers, that solves their problem.'

'Ha, yes,' grunted Commander Hardaport, 'and
if the supermarket doesn't want to lose their custom it will have to cooperate or be blockaded,
dammit!'

Professor Branestawm didn't have much trouble
persuading the supermarket manager, Mr Pryce-

Rize, that his floating supermarket idea was a winner.

'It will be wonderful publicity,' said Mr Pryce-Rize, rubbing his hands together, 'and we shall, of course, get a lot more customers because at present many of the people who live in River Lane get their groceries from other shops. But if we cruise our floating supermarket to them we shall be sure to get their custom. Excellent, excellent!' And he went away to put up the price of tinned bread pudding and frozen Irish stew.

Professor Branestawm's floating supermarket came puffing down the River Pag with all flags flying. Commander Hardaport (Retired) was at the helm, steering a careful course among the ducks, who had gathered in case there was any free food going, and avoiding the hire cruisers who didn't seem to know their port from their starboard.

'Hurray!' cried all the bungalow dwellers in River Lane, who had lined up in their gardens at the edge of the river.

The floating supermarket drew up with a hiss of steam and a great deal of going astern and nautical shouts from Commander Hardaport.

The Professor had created this astonishing vessel from an old steamer with a couple of disused greenhouses fastened on top, several assorted awnings and nine masts to accommodate all the flags of the Common Market, although this was certainly a very uncommon market.

To shop at Branestawm's floating supermarket, you went aboard at the bows, or up front, as un-nautical people called it. But instead of having to walk round the shelves as in an ordinary supermarket, you sat on a comfortable, sea-going chair and the shelves came to you, rolling past nice and slowly so that you had plenty of time to choose what you wanted. And if you missed something you only had to wait and in due course it would come round again. (It was like Professor Branestawm's method of finding his way at traffic roundabouts, where he kept going round until he recognized somewhere on a signpost. Usually it was the way back home so he didn't often get far.)

You didn't have to carry your shopping round in a wire basket or tin pram, you simply dropped the things on the floor and they rolled along special channels to the stern, where they were gathered up and your bill was made out. All the shopping was then hoisted on a nautical crane, swung over and landed on shore, where you had to be ready with your shopping basket. Right across the deck was a great banner, edged with Union Jacks and a patriotic message saying 'Buy British'. And among the things the supermarket sold were: French bread, Danish pastries, Brussels sprouts, German sausage, Swiss rolls, Dutch cheese, Spanish onions, Viennese fancies, Chinese figs and Belgian buns. Gangways were lowered. Cries of delight went up and the housewives of River Lane swarmed like joyous bees on board the supermarket.

Mr Pryce-Rize was delighted. He had never been rushed at by so many eager customers before. He took reckless tuppences off recommended prices right and left. He made special offers on the spur of every moment. He created baskets full of bargains fore and aft.

Mrs Flittersnoop, always a careful shopper, bought nothing at all because it was so cheap she felt she didn't need it. But Mrs Trumpington-Smawl stocked up with so much she had to sleep in the kitchen because her bedroom was full of groceries.

'I really do, er, feel that I have contributed something to the welfare of the district,' said Professor Branestawm at breakfast next morning.

'Yes, indeed, sir,' agreed Mrs Flittersnoop, handing him a fried egg which he put in his pocket.

Even the Pagwell police were glad about the Professor's floating supermarket, because it meant fewer cars parked in the High Street.

But trouble was on the way.

The River Pag Controllery heard about the Professor's supermarket, felt sure there was a by-law against it and immediately made one in case there wasn't. Then they sent their second-best launch, flying a pink and orange spotted flag, to stop it.

'Heave to there!' they shouted, as they approached the floating supermarket.

'Stand off there, and give us clear passage!' bellowed Commander Hardaport.

'No trading allowed on the river!' yelled the Pag Controllery men.

'Tuppence off recommended price!' shouted Mr Pryce-Rize, throwing a damaged packet of flour at the Pag Controllery launch.

'You are committing an offence against regulation number eighty-five, clause ten, paragraph five!' shouted the Controllery men, coming alongside the supermarket.

'Stand by to repel boarders!' roared Commander Hardaport.

The Supermarket staff opened fire with mince pies, sausage rolls and frozen haddock.

Then the customers on shore came in with reinforcements and attacked the Controllery men with the week's shopping.

*Bong, plop, plop, smack, slosh!* Groceries of all kinds, paid-for and unpaid-for, rained round the launch. The Controllery men waved documents. One of them climbed on the roof of the launch but the supermarket staff scored a direct hit on him with some of last week's eggs. The launch went about and shot up the river making too much wash and so infringing its own regulations.

'Hurray, victory!' shouted the supermarket staff and the River Lane customers.

'Dear me,' said the Professor next day, 'I really had no idea that my idea for helping the housewives would cause so much, er, to-do.'

A few days later the floating supermarket was joined by boats from other shops in Pagwell that thought they might as well do a bit of trade down River Lane. There were butchers' boats, chemist craft, stationery steamboats that weren't at all stationary, vegetable vessels, and hardware barges. Ye Olde Bun Shoppe had a tea clipper that sold tea and olde bunnes. Ginnibag & Knitwoddle's sent a sort of department store ship with several decks and lifts going up and down with girls calling out, 'First floor ladies underwear, blouses and skirts, sports goods and confectionery. Second floor books, boots, boats, bargains of all kinds.' Dr Mumpzanmeazle came tearing along in a narrow punt with an outboard motor, loaded up with pills in case anyone was seasick, and the Vicar had a sort of ecclesiastical skiff rowed by his twin daughters Maisie and Daisie, in very fetching nautical suits. But none of the boats would keep still long enough for him to get a service going so he hoisted suitable prayers on signal flags.

'I had no idea,' gasped Professor Branestawm. It was the second day he had had no idea, which was so unusual as to be almost impossible. 'I had no idea this was going to happen, but at least nothing has gone wrong with my invention.'

It certainly hadn't. The floating supermarket was doing a roaring trade. At least it was doing good trade and Commander Hardaport was doing a great deal of roaring. People who didn't live in River Lane at all and had no need of floating supermarkets, came miles to buy their groceries there because it seemed good fun. And soon the supermarket and the other shopping boats were joined by hire cruisers, packed with people on holiday, determined to enjoy themselves whether they liked it or not.

They bought everything they could possibly need on a river cruise and a lot of things they couldn't, such as garden tools and telephone directory covers.

Suddenly Commander Hardaport, on the bridge of the floating supermarket, roared, 'Enemy approaching on the starboard bow!'

It was the Pag Controllery, a whole fleet of them. They had brought every launch they possessed, led by their very special flagship launch, in which were all the Directors of the Pag Controllery, in their best clothes, sitting round a table in the cabin drinking port to fortify themselves for the battle ahead.

'Heave to and give yourselves up!' shouted a Controllery man.

'Approach at your peril!' shouted back Commander Hardaport.

The launches fanned out as much as the river would let them. They bore down on the supermarket with fists shaking and teeth bared.

'Open fire!' roared Commander Hardaport, letting fly with a giant-size packet of supervitamin breakfast cereal.

One of the launches attacked with a hose, pumping water from the river and aiming it at the supermarket.

The supermarket customers replied with special offers of all kinds.

Then one of the launches collided with the supermarket and dented it in the side.

That did it. No Branestawm invention was going to put up with being dented by a launch. It swung round and the whole of the food distributing machinery let go a terrific broadside. Enough cut-price groceries to feed the whole of Pagwell for a month descended on the Pag Controllery fleet. The Directors' port was washed overboard on the starboard side. Packaged dinners and oven-ready chickens rained down on the decks. The Chief Pag Director was knocked flat on his back and his top hat filled with raspberry essence and pickled onions.

The Controllery fleet reformed and came bearing down on the supermarket. The supermarket fired off a hundredweight of pre-packed luncheon meat and ran aground.

'Gotcher!' yelled the Pag Controllery men.

'Nothing of the kind!' cried Professor Brane-stawm rushing up. 'At this moment we are not trading on the river, we are trading on land. This vessel is aground and therefore no longer subject to your rules.'

'Pah!' snorted all the Pag Directors.

'And what is more,' cried the Professor, 'as this vessel is aground it is now a wreck within the meaning of the Act and it is your responsibility to remove it as it constitutes a danger to shipping. Pray proceed.'

The Controllery men looked at one another. They looked at their Directors, who looked back. They scratched their heads.

'We have no appliances for removing wrecks of that size,' grunted the Directors. 'We are equipped only for removing wrecked punts and derelict dinghies.'

'Well,' said the Professor, 'are you going to re-

'Open fire!' roared Commander Hardaport

move this wreck or are you going to, hrrm, leave us in peace to go about our lawful occasions?'

The Pag men waved their hands. They gnashed their teeth. They stamped their feet. But they were beaten and they knew it. Slowly they went about and chugged off, leaving Professor Branestawm and his now non-floating supermarket to go on selling delicious groceries of all kinds to the gleeful and grateful customers of River Lane.

And, as a celebration, Professor Branestawm invented a special fast-colour non-running blancmange powder for Mrs Flittersnoop, who made it into a bright scarlet blancmange that changed colour four times during dinner and finished up as a heliotrope and lime-green sherry trifle.

Neither the Professor nor his guests, Commander Hardaport (Retired), Colonel Dedshott and the Vicar, had the pluck to eat any, which was just as well as it blew up half an hour later. But fortunately Mrs Flittersnoop had put it out in the garden as it was giving off undesirable smells.

# 5

## The Professor in a Fog

PROFESSOR BRANESTAWM came out of the Elegantique Cinema in Pagwell High Street, where he had gone by mistake for the Museum of Notable Scientific Discoveries, without making the not very notable discovery that it was really a cinema.

'Ha, hum,' he said to himself, 'I really do not think much of the modern scientific film. There seems to be no, ah, logical reason why cowboys shooting at bottles in a public house while ladies with tall hair-dos hide under the tables should be regarded as a notable scientific discovery.'

And thinking like that he came out into Pagwell High Street.

But it wasn't there. The High Street had disappeared.

'Good gracious!' cried the Professor, trying various pairs of spectacles to see if they made the High Street come back. 'Can this be a deep plot by foreign enemies to steal our country's towns and make away with them to distant parts?'

But it wasn't. It was simply an extremely foggy evening. The very grandfather and second cousin of a fog. Nothing could be seen but whiteness and a lot too much of that. It was as if someone had rubbed out Pagwell High Street like a drawing, and left just the white paper.

'Ah, um,' said the Professor, trying to part the fog with his hands. 'I must write a treatise on the causes and nature of fogs and their different varieties. Let me see,' he murmured, 'there is the old-fashioned pea soup fog. There is the Scotch mist type imported from the Highlands and the Pagwell Porridge type, which is what we seem to have here.'

He turned his collar up as far as it would go, which was about one tenth as high as he would have liked it to go because he had put Mrs Flittersnoop's winter dressing-gown on instead of his overcoat.

He walked carefully along the path, bumped into a letter-box, said, 'I beg your pardon, Madam,' saw it was a letter-box and not a fat lady in a red coat with her mouth open, and said, 'Sorry, letter-box,' as he didn't want to quarrel with the Post Office because of the risk of parcels going to the wrong address.

At last, after losing himself fifteen times the Professor finally found himself in the road where he lived, or at least in the road where his house was, because naturally a gentleman of Professor Branestawm's standing didn't live in the street.

'Thank goodness the house next but one to mine is for sale and there's an enormous board on a post in the front garden. I shall be able to find my way home easily. Here we, um, are. That's the *For Sale* board, though I can only just make it out in this fog.'

He groped his way up to the front door, started

looking for his key and remembered he had forgotten it.

He was just going to ring the bell when he remembered too that Mrs Flittersnoop had gone to stay with her sister Aggie in Lower Pagwell.

'I have no doubt the fog will have prevented her from coming home,' he murmured.

'Dear, dear!' said the Professor, looking round but still seeing nothing but fog. 'I really don't know what to do. I'm locked out of my own house in an, er, er, fog and . . .'

He leant miserably against the front door.

It opened.

'Good gracious!' exclaimed the Professor, getting up off the door mat where he had fallen. 'This is most, er, most . . . Mrs Flittersnoop must have forgotten to fasten the door. Or can thick fog open doors?' The Professor began to plan a highly scientific talk on the possible effect of different kinds of fog on the mechanism of door locks under night-time conditions. But suddenly he heard noises. Someone was in the house.

'Ah, er, hum,' he whispered. 'Who can that be? It isn't me, because I'm here. It can't be Mrs Flittersnoop or she'd have put a light on. Ha, it must be a burglar. I must telephone Colonel Dedshott for help. But no, the burglar would hear me and might shoot me. Perhaps I could run quickly to fetch Commander Hardaport (Retired) from next door. But no again, it is too foggy to run quickly anywhere and anyway this is the Commander's night for talking about spinnakers at Pagwell Yacht Club.' Goodness knows how the Professor managed to remember all that when he couldn't even remember his door key, but it's surprising what you can do under sudden strain.

The Professor crept into the hall.

'I shall tackle him with this Diddituptite native club hanging on the wall by the stairs,' he thought. He reached out his hand. There was no club there.

'Oh, my goodness!' gasped the Professor. 'The burglar must have taken it. Perhaps even now he's waiting round the corner to hit me with it.' He slid up the stairs to get to his bedroom, where he kept an old Spaglonian tree-chopping axe night and day for just such an emergency as this.

But as he went up the stairs he ran into something soft coming down.

'Ha!' he gasped. 'Miscreant! Criminal! Breaker-in to other people's houses!' He grabbed at the soft something, which let out gasps of its own. There was the most terrific and invisible struggle on the stairs. It was too foggy outside and too dark inside for anyone to see anything. At last the Professor managed to get the someone down the stairs, across the passage and out through the front door, with the loss of only two pairs of spectacles and his hat.

*Squelch!* The someone landed in a very wet puddle and Professor Branestawm went back into the house and switched the light on.

'Oh, my goodness gracious!' he cried. 'No wonder

I couldn't find the Diddituptite club on the wall. This isn't my house. I recognize it by the stains on the wallpaper made by my last invention, which aren't there.'

He thought for a moment.

'Well,' he said to himself at last. 'I may be in the wrong house but I've certainly done the right thing in throwing a burglar out. The people who live here will be glad.'

But as a matter of fact the person who lived there was anything but glad. He was Mr Marmaduke Mushington Mobley, the Professor's neighbour, and it was he the Professor had thrown out.

For what the Professor hadn't realized was that the *For Sale* board for the house next but one to his was in a corner of the front garden so that it came between two houses. The Professor should have counted the house just after the board as the empty one but, with all the fog about, he counted the one just *before* the board. So instead of going into his own house he went into the one next door to his by mistake. And that was the house of Mr Marmaduke Mushington Mobley, who was a rather new Pagwell Councillor, and who was now sitting in a puddle and thinking that being thrown out of his own house didn't really come under the duties of a Councillor.

'But perhaps this isn't my house,' he said to himself, wishing the puddle he had been thrown into wasn't such a wet one. 'Now I come to think of it I couldn't find the light switch and I know where it is in my house.'

As a matter of fact, he couldn't find the light switch because the Pagwell Electricity Board had been doing some re-wiring in his house and had moved the switch.

'I'd better go down the road and find my own house,' he said. 'I could do with a cup of tea after all that.'

He went groping down the road, while Professor Branestawm carefully switched off the light and closed the door behind him, which was quite unlike the Professor so perhaps the fog had got into his head a bit.

'My, er, house must be farther down the road,' he muttered. Ghostly shapes swam out of the fog to meet him. Trees disguised as spectres loomed up and loomed down again. At last the Professor came to his own house.

'This certainly looks rather like my house,' he said. 'But then it is so difficult to see anything in this fog.'

He went up to the front door, pushed it open and went inside. But no sooner was he inside the house than an invisible someone flung himself on him and threw him out, though fortunately not into a puddle as there wasn't one handy.

'Oh, my goodness gracious!' exclaimed the Professor. 'This can't be my house after all and whoever lives there evidently thought I was a burglar. Dear, dear, now I wonder where I do live? Ah, I will inquire next door and find out where I am.'

He rang the next-door bell and the door was

opened by a gentleman whom he had never seen before.

'Excuse me,' said the Professor, 'but can you tell me where Professor Branestawm lives?'

The man gave him a funny look, which was quite unnecessary because the Professor already had a funny look, with no hat and Mrs Flittersnoop's dressing-gown and fog making him all misty and damp.

'But you *are* Professor Branestawm,' said the man. 'I recognize you. I saw you at a lecture you gave recently in West Pagwell.'

'Tut, tut,' spluttered the Professor. 'I didn't ask you if you knew Professor Branestawm, I asked you if you know where he lives.'

'Now then what's all this, hey, what?' cried a very salt-water voice, and who should come to the door but Commander Hardaport (Retired).

'Ha, Professor Branestawm!' he cried. 'Glad to see you, though this damn fog makes it very difficult. Meet my friend Sydney Yardarm, Assistant Deputy Acting Temporary Secretary of Pagwell Yacht Club.'

'How do you do,' said the Professor politely, trying to raise his hat, which he couldn't do as he had lost it up the road. 'I'm afraid I have lost my way in this, ah, fog,' he said. 'I went to my house next door but it wasn't my house and the person who lives there threw me out, evidently, um, imagining I was a burglar.'

'You must have gone the wrong way,' boomed

*An invisible someone flung himself on him*

Commander Hardaport. 'Your house is on the pòrt
side of my house, you must have gone starboard.
The one on that side has been empty for weeks, so
don't understand why you found someone there.
Could have been a tramp sheltering from the fog.'

'Ah,' said the Professor. 'Very possible.'

He went slowly out into the road, trying to remember which was port and which was starboard.
He groped his way back to what was really his own
house and ran bump into Mr Marmaduke Mushington Mobley who was just coming out. There was a

bit more struggling until they both suddenly fell into a holly bush but got out of it again even more suddenly.

'May I ask what you were doing in my house?' asked the Professor.

'I, er, oh, yes,' said Mr Marmaduke Mushington Mobley. 'I'm so sorry, it's this fog, you know. I thought it was my house. I threw somebody out of it a little while ago who was obviously a burglar.'

'Fancy that!' said the Professor. 'I just went into somebody else's house by mistake and had to throw out a burglar there.'

'Good gracious!' exclaimed Marmaduke. 'And somebody threw *me* out of a house farther up the road which I am sure was my house. It must have been the same burglar. Quick, let's hurry back and we'll catch him!'

But they could only hurry very slowly because of the fog and when they got to the other house there was no burglar there.

'We must, ah, fetch the police,' muttered the Professor. 'The place is knee-deep in burglars. I was just thrown out of *my* house by one. It must be this fog. Um, very interesting. I must plan a paper on the question of whether fog encourages burglars or whether there is something in the theory that burglars are actually a product of fog.'

'Just a minute!' cried Mr Marmaduke Mushington Mobley. 'I think I'm beginning to see it all.'

'I don't see how you can see anything in this fog,' grunted the Professor.

'Listen,' said Marmaduke. 'This is my house. I know it is now. You thought it was *your* house and that I was a burglar, so you threw me out.'

'Tut, tut,' said the Professor. 'I must really be more careful.'

'Now,' said Marmaduke Mushington Mobley, ticking points off on his fingers. 'I then went down to your house, which I thought was *mine* and when you arrived at your own house I threw you out.'

'That is, I fear, no excuse,' said the Professor.

'Well, everything is quite clear now,' said Marmaduke, although it wasn't as the fog hadn't lifted. 'But you must come and have supper with me to make up for my throwing you out of your own house.'

'No, no, nothing of the kind, my dear sir,' said the Professor. 'You must come and have supper with *me* to make up for my throwing *you* out of *your* house.'

They were just about to start a long, complicated argument when Colonel Dedshott slowly materialized out of the fog like a ghost at a magic show, with his horse walking beside him because he thought it might be dangerous to ride horses in fogs.

'Ah, Branestawm, lost in the fog, what!' he cried.

'Er, yes,' said the Professor, 'and allow me to introduce a fellow foggist.'

But Colonel Dedshott knew Mr Marmaduke Mushington Mobley already so introductions weren't necessary. Then they all went back to Colonel Dedshott's house for a nice military supper, because Colonel Dedshott's horse knew the way even in the fog and they just walked behind him, the Colonel holding the horse's tail, Professor Branestawm holding the Colonel's hand and Mr Marmaduke Mushington Mobley holding the Professor's hand.

*Colonel Dedshott's horse knew the way*

# 6

## Musical Housework

FROM Pagwell church hall could be heard the tinkling sound of *The Bluebells of Scotland* being played on the church hall piano. It was followed by *Home, Sweet Home* with only six mistakes, and then the *Minute Waltz*, which took a quarter of an hour.

Was it Professor Branestawm trying to invent the piano into some curious engine? Were piano tuners working to rule? No, it was Mrs Flittersnoop, keeping her hand more or less in on the piano.

'Oh dear,' she said to herself, after an extra doubtful B flat among the sharps, 'I do wish the Professor had a piano. It is so inconvenient, I'm sure, coming here twice a week to practise, and then only if the Girls' Friendly Society or the Men's Ludo Club aren't using the hall. But there,' she added, carefully closing the piano. 'Even if the Professor had a piano I shouldn't really have time to play it, what with all the housework to do.'

As a matter of fact Professor Branestawm had had a piano in his house some years ago. But he had invented most of it into marmalade-detecting devices and things for fishing things out from under the bed. He had also used up a lot of it trying to invent a way of doing the washing-up before dinner instead of afterwards. 'You see,' he had explained to Mrs Flittersnoop, who knew enough about washing up after dinner not really to need it explained, 'you can enjoy your dinner much more if you know you haven't got to wash up afterwards.' But, even with the help of nine-tenths of a piano and a lot of his own particular forte, the Professor couldn't do it.

'The only thing would be,' he said, 'to leave the washing up after dinner and do it next day before dinner.' But that didn't work because some of Mrs Flittersnoop's gravy was rather on the tenacious side and it took chisels and coarse glasspaper to get it off the plates once it had really dried on. In fact, the plates came off the gravy, in bits, more easily than the gravy could be got off the plates.

And after all this, all that was left of the piano was the soft pedal, the key of C sharp split down the middle, and a lot of very noisy and not very well-behaved wire.

'Mrs Flittersnoop,' said the Professor, when she arrived back from her piano practice, 'I, um, er, have been thinking.'

'Yes, indeed, I'm sure, sir,' said Mrs Flittersnoop, remembering that her sister Aggie would be away on holiday for a week or two and wondering where she could go in case this meant disastrous inventions.

'I think it is too much for you to have to go down to the church hall to practise the piano. I think we should have one here.'

'Oh, that is kind of you, I'm sure, sir,' said Mrs

Flittersnoop. 'But I'd be tempted to neglect the housework once I started playing it, I'm afraid.'

'Tut, tut,' said the Professor, waving spectacles all over the place. 'I have, of course, um, ah, thought of the possibility of a struggle between the calls of music and er, more mundane matters of mere housework. And,' he put his spectacles on in the wrong order and looked through three pairs at once, 'I have an idea for combining the two.'

Mrs Flittersnoop folded her hands and prepared to expect the worst without having any idea what it might be. But she had her hair tied back nice and tight and felt ready for almost anything.

'One has various machines for doing the housework,' went on the Professor, 'such as vacuum, um, um, cleaners and dish, er, washers. One also has machines for producing music such as pianos, some of which, I believe, can almost play themselves.'

'Yes, indeed, I'm sure, sir,' said Mrs Flittersnoop, pushing a hair slide in a bit tighter.

'Then why not,' cried the Professor, flinging his arms out and knocking a china vase full of odd buttons, safety pins and used stamps off the mantelpiece, 'why not combine the two? Why not have a machine on which you can play music, so arranged that the action of playing the music can be transferred into other actions which will do certain types of housework?'

Mrs Flittersnoop said nothing.

It was some time before the Professor got his new

invention for musical housework really running in
top gear.

'We must begin with something quite simple,' he
said to Mrs Flittersnoop, 'such as a means of per-
mitting the scale of A major when played slowly to
run a mop over the kitchen floor.'

'Well,' said Mrs Flittersnoop, remembering that
the kitchen floor was covered cooker to sink with a
special carpet the Professor had invented, which was
supposed to clean itself.

'Then,' went on the Professor, getting his spectacles mixed up with the machinery he was working
on and seeing several things wrong inside that he
hadn't known about, 'after that we can proceed to
the more, ah, complex business of arranging *Stran-
ger in Paradise* to dust the cobwebs off the ceiling.'

Eventually the machine was ready for its first test-
ing run. Mrs Flittersnoop seated herself rather gin-
gerly on a piano stool that resembled the driving-
seat of a helicopter and faced the houseworking
piano.

It had the usual row of black and white keys with
a few extra ones in different colours. There were
switches up the sides and levers down the middle
and wheels within wheels on top.

'The piano is connected to a number of housework machines,' said the Professor. 'These,' he went
on, pointing to the coloured keys with the wrong
end of a pair of spectacles, 'are the housework task
selection keys. If you wish bedrooms to be cleaned
you press the blue key but if it is the dining-room

that is to be the subject of housework it is the red key that must be depressed.'

'Yes, indeed, I'm sure, sir,' said Mrs Flittersnoop, wondering if perhaps she was the one that was going to be depressed.

'The music must then be selected,' went on the Professor, rummaging about among albums of popular Victorian ballads and sheets of Top Ten tunes. 'This must be chosen according to the particular task to be carried out. It would of course be quite useless, for instance, to play *A Room with a View* if one wished the bedroom carpet to be cleaned as there is, um, ah, no appreciable view from that point. On the other hand,' he went on, waving both hands, 'should you wish the rubbish pail to be taken from the kitchen and emptied in the, um, ah, municipal refuse container, then obviously *My Old Man's a Dustman* would be an appropriate choice.

'These levers control the extent and amount of work to be done. You would not I, er, imagine,' he said, 'wish the bedroom, for instance, to be continued to be dusted after all the, er, um, dust had been removed?'

'No, indeed, I'm sure, sir,' said Mrs Flittersnoop, who had never yet come anywhere near being able to remove all the dust from the Professor's bedroom, not to mention the old bolts and nuts and bits of escaped invention that were always lying about.

'Just sit down at the instrument,' said the Professor, 'and try out a simple piece of, er, er, er . . .'

Mrs Flittersnoop spread her hands over the key-

*Mrs Flittersnoop spread her hands over the keyboard.*
*'I think we'll try cleaning the stove,' she said*

board. 'I think we'll try cleaning the stove,' she said.

The Professor pressed a coloured button and pulled a few mixed levers. She played *You're the Cream in my Coffee*, as that was the nearest thing she could think of to stoves. There were some whizzings and clanks from out in the kitchen and a trolley slid in with two cups of coffee and a jug of cream on it.

'Ah!' cried the Professor, clapping his hands and bending the spectacles he was holding. 'Not bad, not bad at all, but I fear not quite the most suitable, um, ah, tune.'

Mrs Flittersnoop drank the coffee while the Professor oiled the machine with the cream. Then she tried again.

*Amazing Grace* produced an unexpected visit from Gracie Gorblestone from up the road who was certainly amazed to see what was happening and forgot to ask for the mincer she had come to borrow.

Mrs Flittersnoop played a few bars of *Sunrise, Sunset* which brought all the blinds down. *Tie a Yellow Ribbon round the Old Oak Tree* caused some rather frantic gardening to occur. *Don't Be Afraid of the Dark* turned the lights on all over the house, while a military march brought Colonel Dedshott and the Catapult Cavaliers cantering up to the front door to see if anyone wanted rescuing. But this hardly came under the heading of 'housework' unless you counted the Catapult Cavaliers as household cavalry, which they weren't really.

'The trouble is,' said the Professor, 'to find the

right sort of tune to agitate the right houseworking gadgets.' He was wondering whether he could get some enthusiastic composer to pop out a few hits or at least near misses such as *My heart cries out to have the dining-room spring-cleaned* or *If you love me do the washing up*.

'It's all very clever, I'm sure, sir,' said Mrs Flittersnoop, 'but if I might make so bold as to say so, I couldn't play all these tunes even if I had the music, not without a lot of practice, and it would really take less time to do the housework myself.'

'Ha!' exclaimed the Professor, being suddenly hit by a forty horse-power idea. 'If you are unable to play all these, er, um, tunes yourself, why should we not invite in friends and others who perhaps, like yourself, have no piano on which to practise?'

'Jolly good idea, Branestawm, what, my word,' said Colonel Dedshott. 'And these piano-playing friends could pay a small sum for the use of the piano,' he added. 'Chance of earning a bit of money not to be sneezed at, you know, what!'

'Er, um, yes,' said the Professor, who never sneezed at anything if he could help it because it always brought Mrs Flittersnoop running with boxes of tissues so that he didn't use his handkerchief and so saved the washing.

Next day an announcement appeared in *The Pagwell Gazette* saying 'Modern piano available in private house for practice. Moderate terms. Tea or coffee served.'

*

For the next few days Professor Branestawm's house resounded to the most assorted music while the housework did itself very efficiently though sometimes in rather surprising ways, leaving Mrs Flittersnoop plenty of time when she could have practised the piano if only it wasn't always being used by paying players. And anyway she had all the extra work of getting tea or coffee unless she could persuade the current piano-player to practise *Tea for Two*.

Then one Tuesday Miss Frenzie of the Pagwell Publishing Company arrived with two little girls who wanted to practise for the Great Pagwell Eisteddfod.

'You're always so kind, Professor,' she said, nodding her head and scattering hair grips of all colours among the Professor's spectacles. 'Now come on, children. Start playing and I'll turn over.'

It was all right as long as they kept to *Nymphs and Shepherds, Come Away* as all the nymphs and shepherds within earshot had obviously gone away already. And even *Jingle Bells* produced no noticeable effect except a loud ringing at the front door bell, but that was Commander Hardaport from next door saying why the deuce didn't they play something nautical instead of all this civilian noise.

'Right!' said Miss Frenzie, clamping her hair back with one hand and changing the music with the other.

The little girls took a good sniff each and started *A Life on the Ocean Wave*. Instantly the Professor's bedroom was briskly hosed down and his dressing-table polished with naval smartness and brass polish.

The little girls went on to a hornpipe without missing so much as a crotchet and that gummed up all the Professor's plumbing.

'I can't make the tea because the tap won't run,' complained Mrs Flittersnoop, coming out of the kitchen with the teapot in her hand.

Miss Frenzie hurriedly stopped the sea-going music and started the little girls off on *Rock of Ages* because she saw the Vicar coming up the garden path.

Then one little girl, rather bored with all this serious stuff, started playing a selection of Top Ten tunes from the Hit Parade, and the other little girl, determined not to be played down by her friend, let fly with both hands at the storm music from *The Flying Dutchman*. Miss Frenzie cried, 'No, no, dears! Both together, not different tunes. Let's have something we all know!' And she wedged herself in by middle C and crashed out a bit of *Rule, Britannia*.

That did it. The houseworking machines weren't going to be ordered about in three different directions at once, even by Miss Frenzie and two little girls. Enormous feather dusters began rapidly dusting the piano. Glass-washing and carpet-cleaning occurred with lightning speed. Brushes and sideboards and fancy cushions flew about. The air was thick with everything and a great deal too much of it.

Then a band went past outside and the houseworking machines took this as instructions to polish the dining-room walls. Miss Frenzie accidentally turned on the radio which caused the Professor's study to be thoroughly rearranged, with all the furniture upside-down and the curtains on the floor.

Pandemonium took place. Miss Frenzie let out a yell that got the bathroom completely stripped out. The little girls gave up piano-playing and started crying. The housework machines retaliated by cleaning the windows with cooking fat and Mrs Flittersnoop's cries of anguish only caused the stair carpet to roll itself up and go bounding and bumping down the road, where it met Commander Hardaport broadside on and shipwrecked him on a traffic island.

'Dear me, tut, tut, and good, er, gracious!' cried the Professor, dashing up the garden path and leaving the Vicar to say some suitable prayers for dealing with the situation if he could think of any.

'Stop the music!' cried the Professor, as the radio roared out *Among my Souvenirs* and the housework machinery began dusting Mrs Flittersnoop's favourite ornaments none too gently.

The Professor pulled levers and turned wheels, he unswitched switches and pressed buttons. But as fast as he got the houseworking machinery tamed the Vicar set it off again by playing highly-militant music such as *Onward, Christian Soldiers* and *Fight the Good Fight*. Fortunately these brought the Catapult Cavaliers, Colonel Dedshott and Commander Hardaport (Retired) out in force and all hands and feet set to work to get the Professor's house as far back to normal as it had ever been.

'By Jove, sir, this must be stopped!' roared Colonel Dedshott, drawing his sword and accidentally cutting down the curtains the two piano-playing little girls had climbed up for safety. 'Charge!' he yelled. But the Catapult Cavaliers didn't know whether he meant charge the piano, which of course the Professor was already charging for using, or charge the housework machines.

'Avast there!' shouted Commander Hardaport (Retired) in his best force thirty-five voice.

Three policemen and a traffic warden came in to see if they could fine anyone for improper parking and were immediately parked on the sideboard and given silver to polish by the housework machines who were too busy ironing Miss Frenzie's hair to do it themselves.

Catapult Cavaliers and policemen flung themselves at the piano. Professor Branestawm tried to get untangled from the housework machines. Several neighbours called to complain about the noise and were swept into the battle.

But at last the insurgent housework machinery was finally subdued and all music-making devices silenced.

'Now you'll have to invent a machine to clear up all the mess, y'know,' said Commander Hardaport.

'No, indeed, I'm sure not, sir,' said Mrs Flittersnoop firmly, passing round cups of tea.

'I trust you are not thinking of presenting your

remarkable piano to the Church Musical Society,'
murmured the Vicar.

'Um, well, no, not exactly,' said the Professor,
who had just made up his mind that would be the
easiest way to dispose of the piano, or what was left
of it.

But the problem was joyfully solved by the arri-
val of Pagwell's great sports fans, Mr and Mrs
Horace Hokkibats, who leapt on the piano with
shrieks of delight and said it was just what they
wanted for a new game of musical chairs combined
with backwards badminton and a touch of Rugby.

And as they carted the piano away Mrs Flittersnoop was heard to say in a very determined voice
that she had decided to give up the piano and take
a few lessons on the mouth organ, which she could
play with one hand while doing the housework with
the other, when necessary.

# 7

## The Fountains of Branestawm

SOMETHING seemed to be lacking in Great Pagwell.

The new Town Hall with its magnificent tower stood shining and sensational in the market square. The astounding one-way traffic system continued to make all the traffic go round and round like the jam in a Swiss roll in order to get back to where it started. The bridge over the railway had been closed to make it wider, which meant all the traffic had to go via Lower Pagwell, Pagwell Gardens and East Pagwell in order to get to the other side of the bridge without going over it. And no end of men and mighty machines were busy digging holes on both sides of the High Street, to make a subway so that people could cross the High Street to the lovely new Town Hall without either getting knocked down or impeding the rush of determined motor cars, vans, trucks, lorries and bicycles.

But in spite of all this progress, something still seemed to be lacking in Great Pagwell.

'New Town Hall do look fine and all,' said the Agriculture Councillor. 'But reckon as she do need something in front of her to set her off, as you might say.'

'Yes,' said another Councillor. 'Ornamental gardens, for instance.'

'No, no,' shouted two more Councillors, who didn't dig gardens. 'Why not ornamental lily ponds?'

'People might fall in,' objected other Councillors, who didn't fall in with the suggestion.

*The Pagwell Gazette* got hold of the idea and published an article saying there should be public baths in front of the Town Hall, underground, of course, so as not to be too noticeable and added that the subway at present being made could form the entrance to the new baths.

Then sacks full of letters came bursting in from people who thought the idea was fine, those who thought it was frightful, those who thought mid-way between, and those who didn't think at all but weren't going to let that stop them writing to the paper.

'Does Pagwell need public baths?' shouted the next issue of *The Pagwell Gazette*, which had only started the thing to stir up a bit of interest in the paper, as there wasn't much news.

'I don't think we want baths,' said a Councillor. 'But we might perhaps have some public showers.'

'We get enough of them when it rains,' said another Councillor.

Just then their coffee break occurred and, apart from the suggestion that they might build an open air café, which was objected to by those Councillors who didn't want people rushing about with doughnuts in front of their nice new Town Hall, nothing more happened.

Next day there was a quiet tap on Professor Branestawm's back door and Mrs Flittersnoop found the Mayor standing outside with a finger to his lips.

'Is the Professor in?' he whispered.

'Yes, sir,' she whispered back, and the Mayor was shown very silently and secretly into the Professor's study.

'This is quite unofficial, Professor,' he said, gazing furtively around as if he expected to find policemen in the waste paper basket or secret service agents behind the inkpot. 'I wish to consult you about what kind of attraction we could have in front of the Town Hall to sort of set it off, so to speak.'

'Er, ah, um,' said the Professor, unhooking some of his pairs of spectacles from places where he had put them so that he would know where they were.

'The others must not know I've consulted you,' said the Mayor. 'You must put in your suggestion entirely off your own bat. Don't say I asked you.'

'Er, um,' said the Professor. 'But supposing the other Councillors have asked other people for suggestions? It would be, er, rather awkward if you had a great many suggestions and had to use all of them. The Town Hall might be completely hidden behind the very things meant to show it off.'

'You make your suggestion, Professor,' said the Mayor, slapping his chest but not slapping it very hard in case he hurt himself. 'I will see that it is adopted.'

'That will settle this absurd argument about what is to go in front of the Town Hall,' he said to himself. 'Each of the other Councillors will think Professor Branestawm has suggested the idea and they will agree to it, so as not to have to agree to an idea suggested by some other Councillor. But the idea will really be due to me. Ha, ha! How clever I am!'

He pulled his hat over his eyes and went out, banging into Mrs Flittersnoop because he couldn't see where he was going.

Two minutes after the Mayor had left there came another secret tap, at the front door this time. It was the Town Clerk, disguised in a false beard that didn't fit and a pair of dark glasses that wouldn't stay on.

'Nobody must know of this visit,' he breathed at the Professor. 'I want you to make a suggestion for some sort of attraction to go in front of the Town Hall to, er, to, er . . .'

'To set it off?' said the Professor.

'Ha yes, how did you guess?' said the Town Clerk.

The Professor didn't tell him because the Mayor's visit had to be secret.

'Now,' thought the Professor. 'I've got to make two different suggestions for the front of the Town Hall, one for the Mayor and one for the Town Clerk. And which one is going to be accepted and how will they sort it out?'

But he just said, 'Leave it to, um, ah, me.'

The Town Clerk crept secretly away thinking he had been very crafty in getting the Professor to put up a suggestion which he knew the other Councillors would agree to because they thought it didn't come from one of them. And he nearly ran into the

Parks and Gardens Councillor who arrived just as secretly, pretending to be a postman.

He was followed just as craftily by the Treasurer, then the Councillor in charge of drains crept in, and by the time he had gone another Councillor arrived until finally the entire Pagwell Council had called most frightfully secretly to ask the Professor to invent an attraction to go in front of the Town Hall. And each of them was highly delighted with himself because he thought he was going to get an idea accepted without any of the other Councillors knowing they were really accepting something he had started. Councillors have very complicated minds, as if they had been invented by Professor Branestawm.

'This is awful!' groaned the Professor. 'All these people asking me to think of something for the Town Hall and none of them must know the others have asked me. And each one promises to get the idea I invent for him adopted. This means I'll have to invent rows and rows of brilliant ideas and all but one will be wasted.'

Then suddenly he was hit by a splendid thought.

'Ha, I have it!' he cried, as Mrs Flittersnoop brought in a cup of tea and a piece of her home-made Madeira cake. The Professor thumped his desk in triumph, just as she put them down, and the cake flew up, bounced off the ceiling and dropped into the cup of tea which fortunately got all soaked up in the cake.

'I shall invent only one invention,' cried the Professor.

'Yes, indeed, I'm sure, sir,' said Mrs Flittersnoop. She took away the tea and cake and brought him a nice glass of lemonade.

'I shall give the same suggestion to all the Councillors,' said the Professor. 'Each one will be determined to get his idea accepted and whichever one is accepted it will be the one I have suggested. Nothing could be simpler.'

'No, indeed, I'm sure, sir,' said Mrs Flittersnoop, thinking a great many things could be much simpler.

'The only thing is, Dedshott,' said the Professor to Colonel Dedshott, who had dropped in on his way back from somewhere, 'although I need invent only one idea for going in front of the Town Hall, what sort of an idea can I invent?'

'Ha, my word, yes!' grunted the Colonel, having no idea at all.

'How about a fine upstanding flagstaff?' roared Commander Hardaport (Retired), who had come in from next door on his way out to somewhere.

'One of the Councillors suggested underground baths,' said the Professor, 'which I thought was rather stupid as if they were underground they wouldn't be seen. Then another Councillor said how about showers and that gave me an idea.'

'Showers never give me ideas,' cried Commander Hardaport. 'Nasty things, showers. Only make your spinnaker wet.'

'What I say is,' said the Professor, taking no notice of the Commander's spinnaker, 'how about turning the idea upside-down and having the opposite of showers?'

'Opposite of showers is no showers,' said Colonel Dedshott, bringing his military intelligence to bear.

'Um, ah, no, Dedshott,' said the Professor, waving spectacles at him. 'Showers are water coming down so the opposite is water going up . . .' He peered at the Commander and the Colonel with the look of someone asking a riddle to which he knows people know the answer.

'You don't mean fountains?' cried the Colonel and the Commander both together.

'I not only mean fountains,' cried the Professor, triumphantly, 'I mean the very essence and poetry of fountains. I mean such fountains as no man has ever seen before, let alone woman.'

'Ha, yes,' snorted the Colonel, who always let women alone as they scared him a bit.

'Such fountains as will make those in Trafalgar Square look like er, ah, er –' He couldn't think what they would make them look like so he cried, 'Go away, thank you for calling! I must turn my mind to fountains.'

He dashed into his inventory, leaving the Commander to go to wherever he was going when he dropped in on the Professor, and the Colonel to go home from wherever he had come back from.

'Well, gentlemen,' said the Mayor, when the Professor's idea was explained to the Pagwell Council. 'I think this is exactly what we want.'

And all the other Councillors cried, 'Hear, hear!' and 'Yes, yes!' each one thinking he was responsible for the Professor's suggestion.

So the entire Pagwell Council agreed with one another for the first time in history.

'Ah fountains,' murmured the Professor, when he heard that his idea had been accepted just as he knew it would have to be. 'I think perhaps I had better make a model first, just a small one.'

By the following Tuesday the model was ready and stood on the Professor's inventing bench along with several days' cups of tea and pieces of cake and breakfasts that Mrs Flittersnoop had pushed in through the window but hadn't been able to clear away for fear of disturbing the Professor.

'Very nice, indeed, I'm sure, sir,' she said, as the Professor carried the model fountain into the dining-room. She hurriedly covered everything in sight with newspapers and dust sheets and pieces of plastic.

The Professor put the fountain on the dining-table and switched it on. It promptly squirted an ornamental spray all over the ceiling, which Mrs Flittersnoop hadn't been able to cover with anything.

'Er, too high,' murmured the Professor. He turned a knob and the fountain took careful aim at the sideboard, shot water into a bowl full of old envelopes, went on to spray a photo of the Professor's grandpa, shampooed the best silver teapot and then

'Oh, oh, oh, dear me, indeed, I never!' wailed
*Mrs Flittersnoop*

dribbled all over the dining-table as the Professor turned it off again.

The next attempt was rather more exciting. Spinning and revolving jets of water washed down the wallpaper, watered the roses outside the window and laundered the velvet curtains.

'Oh, oh, oh, dear me, indeed, I never!' wailed Mrs Flittersnoop, rushing about with umbrellas and dish cloths.

'It seems to work very well,' said the Professor, patting the fountain, which gave him half a pint of water in his eye in return. 'A few modifications, I think, are all that is called for.' And he carried the model back into his inventory while Mrs Flittersnoop called for help in clearing up the mess, but didn't get any.

It took rather a time for the Professor to get the final fountain finished, what with continually thinking of new and sensational ideas and frequently losing vital bits and every now and then going off at tangents on other inventions. So when at last the actual life-size thing was installed outside the Town Hall it was the middle of winter and the fountain had to be covered with plastic sheets and tarpaulins. This wasn't so much to prevent it freezing as to stop people seeing what it was and so spoiling the surprise.

But at last it was summer and when the rain stopped the great Fountain-Unveiling Ceremony took place.

The Mayor and Councillors were there in their best robes. The Catapult Cavaliers band were there, all wearing their spurs, which they had to wear so as to be able to drive their instruments fast enough to please their conductor, Major Zing Boom. He was a very double-forte, highly allegretto, 'let's get it finished before the music runs out' kind of conductor.

The band stopped for breath. The Mayor made a speech and stopped for breath. Then the great Branestawm fountain was switched on.

'Cool' said everyone.

A single jet of water shot up into the air and came down on the Town Hall roof just where the kitchen chimney was and made the soup the chef was preparing for lunch rather weak. The single jet changed to a whole row of smaller jets, all different colours. They went up and down and round and round. The Catapult Cavaliers band struck up *Pennies from Heaven* and everyone put umbrellas up.

Instantly all the smaller fountain jets died down and an excitable revolving one went round and round, washing the windows of the Town Hall.

'Very good, indeed, I'm sure, sir,' murmured Mrs Flittersnoop sharing her umbrella with sister Aggie and little Esme.

Behind the scenes, which was actually under the scenes because he was in a little underground room, Professor Branestawm turned wheels, opened and shut valves.

The fountain died down completely, then every jet it had in stock shot water of various colours sky high and died down again just as the band of the Catapult Cavaliers ran out of music.

Cheers went up all round and everyone went home delighted and a bit damp.

'Um, ah, ha!' exclaimed the Professor, rubbing his hands but forgetting to put down a slice of cake Mrs Flittersnoop had given him for his tea, which made the carpet a bit crumby. 'A really most successful invention, I think. No troubles this time, no troubles at all. Everything went off very well.'

'Yes indeed, sir,' said Mrs Flittersnoop, passing him a cup of tea and getting out the vacuum cleaner.

For the next week the marvellous Branestawm Fountain was the wonder of the Pagwells. Day and night it spouted and sprayed and squirted all colours of the rainbow and a few the rainbow hadn't thought of. People came miles to see it. The Pagwell Councillors patted each other on the back and increased their salaries.

*The Pagwell Gazette* produced a highly-coloured supplement with photos of the fountains, some of them upside-down but nobody noticed. Everything was as perfect as any Pagwellian could wish.

Ten days later the plumbers came to check the pipes in the Town Hall and found that somebody had been tinkering with the plumbing. They didn't realize that the Professor had connected his fountain to the Town Hall water supply in the kitchen and had got all the pipes mixed.

'We'll soon fix this,' said the plumbers, and mixed the pipes up a lot more.

Outside the fountain suddenly started spouting hot cocoa.

'Good gracious!' gasped the Professor. He rushed into the Town Hall underground workings and got busy with spanners. The fountain gave up hot cocoa and distributed warm paraffin instead. Inside the kitchen the plumbers were hard at work with more and bigger spanners. The supply of paraffin ran out and people who had brought cans to collect it for their oil stoves were served instead with gallons of lime juice and hot tea.

'What's all this?' cried the Mayor, rushing out of the Town Hall in a dither and his best robes.

Professor Branestawm pulled levers and twiddled valves. The fountain gave out boiling tomato soup with currant dumplings. The plumbers decided it was time they had their tea break and went home.

'To the rescue!' roared Colonel Dedshott, dashing up with Catapult Cavaliers.

''Vast heaving!' yelled Commander Hardaport, waving a second-hand cutlass.

The fountain opened fire with sausage rolls and soda water.

People came tearing up with plates and basins and buckets and jelly moulds and flower vases to catch whatever kind of mad food and drink came their way.

Then General Shatterfortz arrived with a battery of extremely bad-tempered guns. *Boom! Zong! Crash! Boom!* they opened fire on the fountain.

*Screeech, bong!* the shells went screaming overhead and missed the fountain by innumerable metres.

The fountain retaliated with very fizzy, ice-cold mulligatawny soup, and then knocked the General's hat off with a well-aimed shot of warm gravy.

'Fire!' roared the General, wiping gravy out of his eyes like a true soldier.

*Squeee, bong!* This time a shell landed on the brand new Pagwell Town Hall and set it on fire.

'All hands to the pumps!' roared Commander Hardaport, throwing a bucket of water at the flames, missing it and sloshing Colonel Dedshott instead.

'Fetch the Fire Brigade,' screamed the Mayor.

But the Fire Brigade wasn't needed. Professor Branestawm's wonderful, incredible, undaunted fountain saw the flames and decided it could do better than that. Revolving jets of clean water swung round. The fountain took aim and thank goodness its aim was better than General Shatterfortz' gunners. *Hissss*, the water landed on the flames. Steam rose up like all the world's washing-days and in fifteen and a half seconds, Pagwell time, the fire was out. The Town Hall was saved, all except the Mayor's best tea towel, which had scorched edges, and several demands for rates, which got burned up so much they couldn't demand anything.

After that Professor Branestawm invented special

portable revolving fountains to equip the Pagwell
Fire Brigade, which thus became the most original
and most efficient fire brigade in the country.

But the main fountain is still outside the Town
Hall. Thanks to some careful work by the Pagwell
plumbers, enthusiastically obstructed by the Professor, the fountain now plays water and nothing
but water but it has lovely coloured lights on it all
night.

# 8

## Branestawm's Garden

MRS FLITTERSNOOP was helping Professor Branestawm weed the garden.

'I, ah, find this weeding business somewhat con-
fusing,' said the Professor, pulling up a flower by
mistake, which gave him such a reproachful look, he
put it back again and patted its leaves. 'For instance,' he went on, 'I, er, find that some of the weeds
with long names are more difficult to pull up than
those with short names. But then on the other hand
there are weeds with very short names that are almost impossible to pull up at all and some with extremely long names that practically pull themselves
up if you look at them severely.'

He transplanted two pairs of spectacles from
among the marigolds into his pocket.

'Yes, indeed, I'm sure, sir,' said Mrs Flittersnoop.
Everyone said Mrs Flittersnoop had green fingers
because flowers liked growing for her. Professor
Branestawm at that moment also had green fingers,
and a green nose and a partly green chin, but that
was because his fountain pen, full of green ink, had
leaked a bit.

'I really think you ought to invent something to
make weeding easier sir,' said Mrs Flittersnoop,

making ouching noises as she straightened up after a short sharp battle with some thistles. 'Something to let you pull weeds up without having to stoop down.'

'Ah, um, yes,' said the Professor, scratching his head and getting earth in his hair because he had forgotten to put down a clump of weeds. 'Perhaps we might just wait until the weeds grow tall so that we can pull them up without bending.'

'Oh, I don't think that would do at all, sir,' said Mrs Flittersnoop. 'Some of these weeds don't grow tall, they sort of spread out all over the ground. Very bad for the flowers, sir.'

'Well, perhaps a specially designed, biologically-slanted semi-hormone-induced, bacterial selective weed-killer is what we need,' murmured the Professor. 'That would kill the weeds but not the flowers.'

'Well, sir, I do hope you'll be careful,' said Mrs Flittersnoop. 'Remember your special fertilizer, sir, that grew such lovely big flowers, but then we had those enormous insects on them. Custard-coloured spiders in bowler hats, I remember, sir, and huge ants with too many eyes. Ugh! You won't do that again, sir, will you?'

The Professor promised he wouldn't and went away to invent some kind of self-weeding garden while Mrs Flittersnoop put away her green fingers and went in to get some sponge fingers for the Professor to have with his morning coffee.

The Professor's first idea was to have a garden

entirely composed of concrete, green for the lawns and black for the flower beds, with brightly-coloured plastic flowers stuck into holes in the concrete.

'They make very realistic-looking plastic flowers nowadays,' said the Professor, 'and my garden would not only not need weeding as there would be no weeds but the flowers would be permanently in bloom, even in the winter.'

Mrs Flittersnoop tried to imagine a concrete garden full of flowers, all sticking up through the snow at Christmas, and failed. And she was just a bit afraid that the Professor's garden might encourage plastic weeds. 'They'd be very, very difficult to get out of the concrete, sir,' she said. But, of course, worst of all was the very idea of plastic flowers, which horrified her nearly as much as the idea of buying cakes instead of making them. 'Plastic flowers in the garden!' she thought. 'What *would* the neighbours say?'

Well, one neighbour was Commander Hardaport (Retired) and he said it was a jolly good idea. 'Make you independent of the weather, you know,' he cried. 'Rain not needed but if it comes it'll wash the dust off the confounded flowers. No petals to fall and make the place untidy. Could be very ship-shape all round.' He added that he thought it would be a jolly seaman-like idea if the Professor would invent some flowers that came up at sunrise and went down again at sunset, as flags have to do, and weren't there some flowers called flags anyway, so what was the Professor waiting for?

The Vicar wasn't so keen. Plastic flowers in church he felt would really be somewhat irreverent. Too un-traditional. The same thought had prevented him from having a tape recorder to replace the organ, which always needed things done to it, or money spent on patching its pipes, or men in to mend its manuals.

'I think it's a marvellous idea, Professor,' cried Miss Frenzie of the Pagwell Publishing Company. 'I wouldn't have plastic flowers in my garden for anything, but it will make a simply tremendous subject for a book. "Gardening without tears, without weeds, without trouble and summer flowers all the year round".' And she shot off to write it which she did by dictating it to her secretary Violet twice as fast as Violet could take it down.

'I really don't know what people want,' said the Professor, shaking his head very slowly so that his five pairs of spectacles wouldn't fly off.

'They want it all ways, by Jove!' grunted Colonel Dedshott, who had called to see if the Professor's concrete garden had possibilities for defending the realm and found it hadn't.

'But I am giving it to them all ways,' protested the Professor. 'A garden always in flower. Weeds always absent. They can sit in the garden always without, um, ah, feeling there is some drastic task that must be done such as getting the garden watered before it rains.'

The Professor's second idea was to have all the flower beds at waist height so that you didn't have to stoop to weed them. But that meant having them on top of little walls and the walls rather hemmed the garden in.

'And, of course, sir,' put in Mrs Flittersnoop, always anxious to be helpful, 'if the flower beds were waist high you wouldn't be able to reach some of the tall flowers and that would mean ladders and things.'

Professor Branestawm was just about to go off into inventing spasms to produce self-erecting, collapsible ladders for weeding waist-high flower beds when he was stopped by another astounding idea.

'Ha!' he cried, clapping his hand to his head. 'This is it! Tut, tut, this will revolutionize gardening!'

He rushed round to Colonel Dedshott, found he had gone out, followed him to the Catapult Cavaliers' drill hall, lost his way, arrived at Pagwell bus station in time to miss the wrong bus and finally got to the drill hall by trying to get to Pagwell Station.

'Ha! My word, by Jove, yes!' cried the Colonel, when he had had the idea described to him. This time it was the Colonel who clapped his hand to his head.

'The flower beds will be in specially constructed trays,' said the Professor. 'They will of course be at ground level as is usual with flower beds.'

'Ha!' grunted the Colonel, trying to say something but not getting a chance.

'And when weeding has to be done,' went on the Professor, taking no notice, 'by a simple mechanism the flower beds are raised to waist height, thus making it easy to pull up the, um, ah, weeds, after which the flower beds return to their normal position.'

'Ha, yes, by Jove!' panted the Colonel, waving his hands in a very un-military fashion. 'But don't you see, Branestawm, your idea has possibilities for defence of the country. By Jove, yes! Soldiers concealed in trenches, to be raised up to fire on enemy, then lowered again out of sight.'

The Vicar was just as enthusiastic about the Professor's idea.

'But my dear Professor,' he beamed, 'this is exactly what we need for the church choir. The choir boys are dear boys,' he spread out his hands, 'but boys will be boys, you know, and I find their actions during my sermon most distracting. Now your idea, Professor, applied to the choir stalls would be perfect. The boys could be raised up to sing the hymns and lowered safely out of sight during the lessons and the sermon.'

'Uh, ah, yes,' murmured the Professor.

Dr Mumpzanmeazle was as pleased as if he had discovered a new kind of illness with square spots.

'Just the thing for the hospital,' he cried. 'Problem with hospital beds is, if you have 'em high enough for doctors and nurses to attend to the patients without bending down, the beds are too high for the patients to get in and out safely. Now your idea, Professor, means they can have their beds at floor level for getting in and out and be raised up to any convenient height for medical attention. Of course, some hospitals have something of the kind already. But with your idea, which is mechanically self-operating, we won't even need any bed-operatives.'

'Ah,' murmured the Professor, beginning to wish he'd invented something that didn't lend itself to being messed about with quite so much.

Mr Pryce-Rize, manager of the supermarket, liked the idea too. He said it would make sure that all the goods could be brought within his customers' reach. Of course some of the prices were out of the customers' reach and the Professor's invention didn't help there.

Mr and Mrs Horace Hokkibats were delighted with the idea. They immediately began working out a wild game of table tennis in which you could suddenly lower the table while your opponent was trying to bounce the ball, then raise it again to stop him getting it over the net.

None of the Pagwell Councillors thought much of the Professor's elevating flower beds, partly because it didn't mean any extra banquets and partly because they couldn't see how it could be used to produce complicated new one-way traffic systems or inter-communicating roundabouts.

But the Pagwell Council Gardeners were all for it. And some of the ex-Gardeners who had left to drive underground trains or do other nice dry, indoor jobs said if the Professor's invention was installed in the parks they would come back and be Gardeners again.

'Um, ah, really, Mrs Flittersnoop,' gasped the Professor, as requests from all these people came in to have his invention installed and adapted here, there and everywhere. 'This is, of course, most flattering but ...' He wandered away into his inventory and set about getting his self-elevating flower beds adapted and installed as secret self-operating military trenches, as self-concealing choirboys stalls, as adjustable hospital beds, as up-and-down supermarket shelves, as larky table-tennis tables, as well as installing them in Pagwell Park as flower beds.

It took a bit of doing, but he did it. The Branestawm spirit was up. Was he, the inventor of more world-shaking ideas than the world could stand, going to be beaten by a mere set of ups and downs? Never. A thousand and one times no!

'What a very excellent idea,' cooed the Mayoress, inspecting Professor Branestawm's elevating flower beds in Pagwell Park. 'Saves all that bending down when weeding.' And she bent down to smell a flower.

Perhaps there ought to have been notices saying, 'Don't smell the flowers', like those that say 'Keep off the grass'. But there weren't. It was a pity because this particular flower shot up and hit the Mayoress on the nose.

'Good gracious!' she exclaimed.

The flower bed had elevated itself to the weeding position, then, finding nobody seemed inclined to weed it, it sank down again.

'Switch off the mechanism!' cried the Town Clerk hurriedly.

Somebody pulled a lever.

'Stop!' cried the Professor. 'Unauthorized persons must not interfere with the mechanism. I will make any, um, ah, necessary adjustments.'

He pushed the lever back.

The Town Clerk grabbed it and pulled it over again.

'No, no!' cried the Professor, pushing it back.

*Click, clock, clank!* The Professor and the Town Clerk waggled the important lever as if they were stirring Christmas pudding.

They shouldn't have done.

Professor Branestawm's self-elevating flower beds weren't prepared to be treated like that. They began rising and falling, going faster and faster. Lumps of earth flew off and landed in the Mayoress's hat. Weeds shot out without waiting to be pulled up.

At that very moment the Vicar was preaching a quiet sermon in his quiet church.

'Life is full of ups and downs,' he said.

Instantly a pewful of quiet choirboys shot up from their hideout. The boys thought it was time for the next hymn and burst into *Lift up your hearts and be lift up*. Instantly the pew sank down again. Disembodied voices rose up from unseen depths, *Out of the deep I call*. The Vicar tried to go on with his sermon but had lost his place. Then the choirboys shot up into view again, got in five bars of *Above the clear blue sky* and went down again at once. Up, down, up, down.

Mrs Flittersnoop, who had come to the service as

*Shot up into the air like anti-aircraft shells*

it was Wednesday and the shops were shut, cried, 'Oh my goodness, indeed, I'm sure!'

Up and down shot the choirboys. One of them threw a chunk of bubblegum into the works, which made things much worse. The Verger rushed round with the collecting plate in case people got away before he could reach them.

Meanwhile in Pagwell Hospital a rather nervous student nurse clapped a sticky dressing on a patient. But the bed went *whizz, clank* down and she stuck half of it on herself and half on the doctor she was helping.

*Whizz*, the bed shot up again and tipped the stuck-together nurse and doctor on to the next bed, which promptly went down and tipped them off on to the floor. Beds to right and left shot up and down. Staff nurses tried to administer soothing pills but didn't know where to put them.

On the Catapult Cavaliers' parade ground a detachment of Cavaliers, lying in one of the Professor's self-elevating trenches, were shot up into the air like anti-aircraft shells.

In the supermarket groceries of all kinds began going up and down so fast nobody knew what the cost of living was. Several customers got swept up with the special offers and were nearly bought at bargain prices.

Back in Pagwell Park the flower beds were having a riotous time, tossing the Mayoress from the geraniums to the dahlias and back to the marigolds. Mr and Mrs Hokkibats would have loved to see it only they were being batted to and fro like one of their own ping-pong balls by their self-elevating table.

Oh dreadful situation! All these people being upped and downed by the Professor's wild invention, and nobody to rescue them. The Catapult Cavaliers couldn't do it this time, for they were being tossed about like pancakes themselves.

But help was at hand from a most unexpected quarter. A traffic warden went into Pagwell Park to see if someone had parked a car on the grass so that she could give them a ticket. She was a very resourceful traffic warden, and when she saw the flower beds whizzing up and down she instantly assumed it was against the traffic laws, whether it was or not. She fetched the police who came tearing up in panda cars, on motor cycles and on foot.

'Now then, what's all this?' they cried, and without waiting for an answer, which the flower beds were too busy shooting up and down to give, they set about them. They arrested the up-and-down movement without any of the usual warnings. They charged the flower beds with committing a breach of the peace. They had a lovely time, until they were disturbed by the Verger from Pagwell church who rushed up calling for help and saying prayers both at once.

The police left the dismantled flower beds and rushed off to Pagwell church, where they released the choirboys, who ran off to fetch the Catapult Cavaliers and arrived just in time to rescue them. But, alas, Colonel Dedshott and the Catapult Cavaliers were denied the privilege of rescuing the people at the hospital. The Chief Surgeon, assisted by an ambulance driver and two cooks, managed to remove a vital part from the rising and falling mechanism and everything stopped for tea.

'Ah,' said the Professor that evening when Mrs Flittersnoop gave him an extended news bulletin about it all. 'If only people would refrain from interfering with the mechanism of my inventions, all would be well.'

'Yes, indeed, sir,' said Mrs Flittersnoop. And as she had the Professor's favourite pudding, and as he actually ate some of it, all really was as well as anyone could expect.

# 9

## *Mrs Flittersnoop's Handbag*

PROFESSOR BRANESTAWM sat comfortably in an armchair, the right way round, with all his five pairs of spectacles neatly arranged, actually drinking a cup of coffee Mrs Flittersnoop had brought him, instead of filling his fountain pen with it. He was feeling very calm and serene. No ideas for astounding inventions were buzzing in his brains. No complicated calculations were occurring in his head.

Mrs Flittersnoop was beginning to get a bit worried and was just going to call in Dr Mumpzanmeazle to see what was wrong with the Professor, when he said, 'I think I shall invent a nice, quiet, simple little invention that will give no trouble to anyone.'

'Yes, indeed, sir,' said Mrs Flittersnoop, fearing the worst.

'Something quite small,' said the Professor. 'No revolving restaurants, no cumbersome machines for this and, um, ah, that. Just something quite personal and easy.'

Mrs Flittersnoop wondered whether she should give him one of her powders just in case. She opened her handbag to look for one.

'Ha!' cried the Professor, dropping his coffee cup into the waste paper basket and scraping his spectacles off. 'The very thing! Of course! Couldn't be better! I shall do it at once.'

'But . . .' protested Mrs Flittersnoop.

'Your handbag, Mrs Flittersnoop,' said the Professor. 'You are always saying you cannot find things in it or that it won't hold this or that.'

'Yes indeed, sir,' said Mrs Flittersnoop, who regarded a handbag as a cross between a lumber room, a furniture warehouse, a first aid kit and a savings bank.

'I shall invent you a handbag,' said the Professor, folding his hands and settling back in the armchair. 'I shall invent such a handbag as the world has never seen. And I shall begin my inventing in a very scientific manner by conducting some research to find out how people regard handbags, what kind of handbags they prefer and the purposes for which they use them.' And he went off to ask his friends handbag questions.

'Handbags!' cried Colonel Dedshott, when the Professor told him of the new invention he was working on. 'Never use 'em, myself. Ladies' stuff, y'know. What!'

'Ah,' murmured the Professor. He noticed that the Colonel had a large satchel kind of bag full of maps to carry on manoeuvres, and another bag to carry his catapult bullets, and still another filled with rations in case he got hungry. Even his horse had a sort of handbag on its saddle containing a spare breakfast. And the Catapult Cavaliers were draped with little handbag arrangements to hold

ammunition and spare socks and bandages and all
the other things soldiers may need when dealing
with enemies.

'Handbags!' cried Dr Mumpzanmeazle. 'What
should I know about handbags? No use for them.'
He picked up the black bag that doctors have to
carry day and night and went off to deal with im-
patient patients.

'Handbags,' said the Pagwell Town Clerk, when
the Professor mentioned the matter to him. 'Nothing to do with me.' He picked up a leather bag with
a lock on it that was supposed to be full of Pagwell
Council documents, but was really full of two sandwiches and a tomato, and went out to have lunch in
the Park.

'Handbags,' murmured the Vicar, opening the
bag on his bicycle and making sure he had his prayer
book and a clean handkerchief in it. 'My dear Professor, I feel you should ask my wife. Handbags are
hardly in my line.' He rode off while the Professor
went into the Vicarage to see what the Vicar's wife
could tell him about handbags. But she was a very
manly sort of lady who wore rough tweed skirts and
jackets with a great many pockets and never used
lipstick or powder or indulged in peppermints or
relied on safety pins or used any of the things Mrs
Flittersnoop always carried about with her.

'Never had a handbag in my life,' she grunted.
'Stupid things. Always getting lost.'

The Professor called on Lady Pagwell to see if she
could tell him anything about handbags but she
wasn't much help either.

'I never carry a handbag,' she said. 'No need to. I never pay cash for anything as I have accounts everywhere and so I don't need to carry money. And everything I need in the way of perfume or lipstick or other odds and ends I keep in the car.'

Miss Frenzie of the Pagwell Publishing Company who was whirling in and out of doors with handfuls of papers shouted, 'I think I had a handbag once. Lost it somewhere. Never use one, though. Too many other things to carry.'

Maisie and Daisie, the Vicar's twin daughters, said they never bothered with handbags. They stuffed anything they wanted in their boyfriends' pockets.

'It's a bit awkward sometimes, though,' said Maisie, (or was it Daisie?) 'when you feel like a peppermint and you find you're out with the boyfriend who has your eyebrow pencil, and the pepermint-lozenge boyfriend has gone off with your twin sister, not knowing it isn't you.'

'Ah, um, er,' muttered the Professor. 'It really seems as if handbags are used only by men and that ladies are not interested in them. But Mrs Flittersnoop always has a handbag, in fact, she has a great number.'

The Handbag Buyer at Ginnibag & Knitwoddle's was very anxious to help.

'Fashions change so much, you know,' she said. 'We have a very wide range of handbags, as you can see.' She waved her hand and knocked two of the Professor's pairs of spectacles into a gaping red handbag that a lady was looking at to see if it had interior

pockets. Finding it had, she shut it up and an assistant whisked it off and wrapped it up. The lady disappeared into the street with it and took a fast bus
to somewhere and the Professor had to put advertisements in the paper to get his spectacles back.

But so far Mrs Flittersnoop was no nearer getting
her wonderful handbag.

That evening Mrs Flittersnoop was reading in
bed. It was a book with very small print. She always
chose those because there was more to read and so it
seemed better value. But she found it rather difficult
to make out the words, even with her best spectacles,
unless the light was good. There was no room for a
lamp on her bedside table, which already had on it a
glass of water in case she was thirsty in the night, an
alarm clock to wake her up in the morning, aspirins
in case of midnight headaches, tissues in case of midnight sneezes, lozenges in case of midnight coughs
and a little tiny electric torch which she could switch
on to see what time it was because she didn't like to
put the main light on in case it woke her up too
much.

So what with all this there was no space for a bedside lamp, and so she had to hold the lamp in one
hand and her book in the other, which made her
look like the Statue of Liberty studying for its A
levels.

But, although her bedtime book had small print,
it had very large situations and was so exciting that
it made Mrs Flittersnoop dream.

She dreamt Professor Branestawm had invented for her the most enormous handbag and they had got lost in it. She clambered over the week's housekeeping money, fell into an unzipped pocket which led into a long plastic corridor full of safety pins and old bus tickets. There she met the Professor and they tried to fight their way out of the handbag by cutting through the sides with a fish knife the Professor happened to have with him. But that only led into another part of the handbag littered with competition forms and sticky non-stick saucepans.

'Really, that is most interesting,' said the Professor next morning, when Mrs Flittersnoop told him about her dream before she forgot it, which she always did unless she told it before the kettle boiled. 'I myself had a not unsimilar dream,' he said, looking at his boiled egg and wondering why hens laid them that shape instead of plain round. 'I dreamt I had invented a handbag for you and we met inside it for tea. After that, er, um, ah –' The Professor found he couldn't remember what he had dreamt after that but as it was a dream about finding a whole houseful of furniture down the sides of an old armchair, perhaps it was just as well he couldn't remember, or he might have had all the armchairs in the place to bits to see if there really was anything down the sides.

But Mrs Flittersnoop still hadn't got her marvellous, world-shaking handbag.

Professor Branestawm stood in his inventory looking at the results of his handbag researches. They consisted of seventeen different handbags, ranging from the tiny and sophisticated, made of gold chain so fine it was hardly there at all, through alluring black velvet handbags, costly crocodile handbags and real leather handbags to gigantic plastic handbags in all the colours of the rainbow.

'I, er, um, ah,' he said. 'It seems to me that what is wanted in a handbag is something that is not too large but which can be opened out to provide accommodation for whatever one desires to, um, ah, put into it.'

But he found that if you had a handbag that could be opened out enough to hold everything a lady wants to put into it, it was too full to be folded up again. And even if you could fold it up it was too fat in its folded state to go under your arm and too awkward to carry any other way.

The Professor then developed a sort of subdivided, extensible handbag that could be taken apart so that only those portions required for the day need be used.

'But then I am, ah, afraid it is possible that Mrs Flittersnoop might want to put into her handbag something for which that part of the handbag she had with her was not suitable.'

He devised a stupendous handbag, so big that if it had had a bathroom you could have lived in it. But the Pagwell Council wouldn't give it planning permission in case it spoilt the amenities of the neighbourhood.

He had five more tries at inventing the ultimate, inexhaustible, collapsible, fold-away, adaptable handbag but succeeded only in collecting so many bits and pieces he began to feel he ought to invent himself a handbag to put them all in.

Mrs Flittersnoop didn't look much like getting her astounding and never-before-thought-of-handbag yet awhile. But she found she could make do very nicely, thank you, with the collection of handbags the Professor had accumulated during his researches. Only she could never quite decide whether a mauve plastic handbag with gold ornaments went better with her best, blue spotted dress than a black velvet one with white fringe and silver tassels. And sister Aggie down at Lower Pagwell was having the time of her life with the most exotic handbag made of imitation leopard skin with imitation tortoise-shell fittings, an imitation snakeskin handle and lined with imitation pink silk. But she had to carry her old black plastic handbag with her as well, because she couldn't bring herself to put anything into the exotic one in case she spoilt it.

Then one stupendous day the Professor achieved his ambition. A handbag such as the world had never seen before. A handbag of all handbags. The handbag wonder of the universe.

'Well, I never did, I'm sure, sir,' exclaimed Mrs Flittersnoop, when she saw it.

'I have, er, noticed,' said the Professor, 'that ladies often have with them a sort of shopping bag on wheels to save them having to carry their shopping.'

'Yes indeed, sir,' said Mrs Flittersnoop, who had often been run into by recklessly-driven shopping carriers.

'My idea is rather better,' said the Professor modestly. 'You not only do not have to carry this handbag, you do not have to wheel it either. It will accompany you under its own power and carry whatever you wish it to carry.'

'Why, it's just like a dog,' said Mrs Flittersnoop, patting the handbag, which was shaggy in places and did look a bit like a dog, especially when it opened its mouth to take in shopping.

'I hope it doesn't bite,' giggled Mrs Flittersnoop.

'Er, no,' said the Professor. 'You just blow this special whistle and it will do whatever you want. Look at this, for example.'

The Professor put a tin of stewed steak on the table and blew his special whistle. The handbag opened itself, picked up the tin, swallowed it and shut itself again.

'When you get home,' said the Professor, 'you blow two blasts.' He blew them. The handbag opened itself, put the tin back on the table and closed itself again.

'Well, that I never did, I'm sure, sir,' said Mrs Flittersnoop.

The self-propelled, self-collecting and delivering handbag was quite a sensation at the supermarket. Mrs Flittersnoop found herself getting a lot of things she didn't really want just to show off the handbag

'Why, it's just like a dog,' said Mrs Flittersnoop

to her friends. But it was all right because she just blew two blasts on the special whistle and the hand-bag put the things back.

'It's quite a pleasure to go shopping now,' she said to the Professor.

Next day she arrived home with her shopping, blew two blasts on the special whistle and watched the handbag unload itself on to the kitchen table.

'Why do we want five family-size packets of desic-cated oatmeal and raisin breakfast food?' asked the Professor, looking at some packets. 'We never eat it.'

'Well no, sir, neither we do,' said Mrs Flitter-snoop, feeling a bit puzzled.

The handbag unloaded two bottles of washing-up liquid of a kind Mrs Flittersnoop wouldn't use be-cause it frothed too much, and six packets of tea she never bought because it gave picture cards of motor cars and her sister Aggie's little girl, Esme, was col-lecting the flower ones.

'I never bought these things,' she cried, looking at her shopping list.

Just then there was a rather truculent knock at the door and two policemen arrived accompanied by Mr Pryce-Rize from the supermarket.

'That's the lady!' he said, pointing at Mrs Flit-tersnoop. 'She took away these things without paying for them.' He pointed to the things on the table. He was a good pointer, was Mr Pryce-Rize.

'I didn't buy these things,' protested Mrs Flitter-snoop.

'Ha, no, you didn't buy them!' cried Mr Pryce-

Rize. 'You certainly didn't *buy* them. You took them and didn't pay for them.'

The larger of the two policemen took out a very small notebook and borrowed a pencil from the other policeman.

'Name and address, please,' he said.

'Tut, tut! Dear, dear!' cried the Professor, looking at them all through various pairs of spectacles in the hope that it would make them go away. 'I am Professor Branestawm and this is my housekeeper, Mrs Flittersnoop, and she certainly did not take things from your shop.'

'Supermarket,' breathed Mr Pryce-Rize, slightly indignantly.

Just then a little boy rode past the house on a new bicycle he had had for his birthday, whistling happily as he rode along. The handbag heard the whistle. It stopped the conversation from getting any more muddled by taking Mr Pryce-Rize's hat and the policemen's helmets and notebook, swallowing them and shutting itself up.

'There now, well I never, indeed sir!' cried Mrs Flittersnoop. 'That handbag, sir,' she said to the Professor, 'it's been taking things I didn't want. It must have heard someone whistling in the supermarket, sir.'

'Do you accuse your handbag of shoplifting?' asked the smaller policeman.

'Arrest it!' shouted the larger policeman.

But the handbag dodged them and was off down the road.

Mr Pryce-Rize leapt into his car, followed by the policemen, the Professor and Mrs Flittersnoop.

The runaway handbag was well ahead by now. It shot past Colonel Dedshott's house just as the Colonel arrived on his horse from a military party.

'Arrest that bag!' yelled the policemen from Mr Pryce-Rize's car.

Colonel Dedshott grasped the situation at once with his military intuition. He reined his horse round and galloped after the car that was tearing after the handbag that was just entering Pagwell High Street.

'After it!' shouted the Colonel, drawing his sword and accidentally cutting a telephone wire.

The handbag shot into Ginnibag & Knitwoddle's just as the Colonel drew up outside, leapt off his horse and collided with Mr Pryce-Rize, the Professor and Mrs Flittersnoop. The two policemen, pausing only to issue a ticket to the car for parking on double yellow lines, dashed into the shop with the others.

Mrs Flittersnoop's handbag was just passing the perfume and cosmetics department when the large policeman blew his whistle.

The bag stopped, grabbed some bottles of expensive perfume and ten boxes of exotic face powder, and then rushed on through stationery, through footwear and into ironmongery.

Both policemen blew their whistles.

The handbag knew what that meant. Two blasts – unload the shopping. It dumped the powder and scent on the counter among hammers and chisels.

One of the bottles smashed to bits and two gentlemen in blue overalls who had been trying to buy a spanner went home smelling so romantic their wives refused to believe they had only been in an ironmongery shop.

On rushed the handbag. The policemen blew their whistles at every turn. The bag grabbed up delicious cakes from the bakery department and dumped them out again among ladies' underwear. *Pheee!* went the whistles. 'Stop thief! Arrest that handbag, by Jove!' shouted Colonel Dedshott.

'I, um, ah, fear this is something I had not anticipated,' panted the Professor.

'Yes, puff, indeed, puff-puff, sir,' gasped Mrs Flittersnoop.

*Pheee!* the handbag selected a huge roll of flowered polyester from the dress materials department and tried to give it to a lady in the garden department, but the whole lot came unrolled and handbag, policemen, Mr Pryce-Rize, the Professor, the Colonel and Mrs Flittersnoop were all entangled in swirling waves of the sort of daisies they didn't cater for in the garden department.

'I arrest, pwouff, you,' gabbled the policemen, struggling with artificial daisies.

Garden assistants, salesmen from men's outfitting and charming girls from perfumes and cosmetics flung themselves into the fray. At last the militant flowered polyester was subdued and the handbag, the policemen, the Colonel, the Professor and Mrs Flittersnoop were sorted out. The policemen tried to handcuff the handbag but it put the handcuffs in its pockets. A garden salesman flung bird netting over it, another one wound hosepipe round it and two helpful girls squirted *Love's Passion Number Eighty-Five* over it.

The handbag was given to Oxfam, who had it made into useful hats for the Diddituptite natives.

That evening, as she brought in the Professor's supper, Mrs Flittersnoop said, 'Well, thank you for your trouble, I'm sure, sir, but I think I'll just manage with my mauve plastic handbag and the black velvet one with the fringe and tassels for best.'

The Professor didn't answer. He was deep in thinking about another nice, quiet, simple little invention that would give no trouble.

## 10

## *The Monstrous Memorial*

In front of Great Pagwell Station, in the middle of the station courtyard, stood a monument. A terrific monument. A highly ornamental and determined-looking pile. A very terror.

It had been there ever since the first Lord Pagwell (the present Lord Pagwell's father) was made a Lord. It had been built, or rather created, erected, put up and devised to commemorate the occasion. It had been designed with savage artistry by the celebrated sculptor, Herr von Phluffenhaar, and constructed with a special kind of ersatz stone invented by Professor Branestawm. The Professor had also invented into it one or two other things which no monument had ever possessed before.

It showed the first Lord Pagwell seated on a sort of throne shaped like the Loch Ness Monster, and surrounded by a set of green and purple mermaids because the first Lord Pagwell had been keen on the sea. Over his head was a fancy canopy to keep the rain off. This was trimmed by festoons of concrete lace and supported by knotted columns, and on top of it all was a kind of super-large family-size ice-cream structure with gilded pineapples.

The first Lady Pagwell didn't think much of it, but she said, if they were going to have it, then there should be a clock on it so that it would be of some use. So a clock there jolly well was. A very Branestawm of a clock that chimed the hours and quarters, told you the date, showed the phases of the moon, marked the temperature and indicated what the weather would be, though it always got it wrong. And at certain times of the day it gave a display of coloured lights and played the favourite tune of the first Lord Pagwell.

'I think it's time we got rid of it,' said the Mayor, at a Council meeting one day. 'It has outlived its usefulness.'

'Pah!' snorted the Drains Councillor, who didn't like the monument because it didn't need any drains. 'Monuments don't live and it never had any usefulness.'

'Oh yes, it did and still does,' protested the Town Clerk. 'It's a very useful place to meet people because everyone knows where it is.'

'It is a traffic hazard,' complained the Head Policeman, who had come to make sure nothing illegal was discussed. 'People run into it at night. If it wasn't there we could park cars there.'

The railway company were all in favour of having the monument done away with. People used to try to buy tickets at it, thinking it was a special cheap-rate tourist office. Others thought it was a waiting-room and wrote rude letters of complaint when they found it wasn't. And visitors to Great Pagwell were known to go inside it thinking it was a hotel and not be able find the way out again, which meant rescuing them with the Fire Brigade. And it kept the sun out of the Station-master's sitting-room.

Lord Pagwell said he would be rather glad to see it go. He thought green and purple mermaids weren't quite in keeping with the dignity of his position and anyway it wasn't his memorial, it was his father's, and besides, Lady Pagwell had scraped a few rather expensive bits off her car on it because she always said she was sure the thing ran into her and not the other way round.

'Well, I, um, ah,' said Professor Branestawm. 'If everyone else wants the memorial removed I shall not stand in the way.' He felt standing in the way of memorial-removers might get him removed somewhere awkward too. 'It is, er, one of my very early pieces of work,' he said, 'done when I was very young and inexperienced, so it is hardly a memorial to my inventiveness.'

So the Great Pagwell memorial was to go. The station yard immediately became full of trucks and bulldozers and men with pickaxes and noisy drills. Would-be passengers couldn't get into the station and had to go round to the other side and come back across the footbridge.

*Bang! Boom! Crash!* The demolition started with great enthusiasm. Day and night the demolishers worked. But at the end of two noisy weeks the memorial looked the same as ever, except that it had a bit more dust on it than usual.

'We can't shift un,' said the Head Demolisher. 'She been and bent all our drills, like, and the lads is getting fed up. One of 'em says as 'ow one 'o them mermaids looks like his mother-in-law and he's afraid to touch it in case it hits back.'

'We had better call in the army,' said the Mayor. 'After all, we've got all those soldiers doing nothing but march up and down. I reckon attacking the memorial would be good practice for them.'

General Shatterfortz was all for it. It meant he could issue orders. He could send round urgent memos. And he did.

The noise of road drills and bulldozers and pick-axers was replaced with the rumble of military wheels and the shouting of military commands. Colonel Dedshott was everywhere at once. The army set about the job in style. First, regiments of army cleaners arrived with buckets and mops and thoroughly cleaned the memorial till it shone like a highly-polished jelly in bright sunshine. Then military painters arrived and touched up the paint. They re-gilded the gold pineapples, they made the whole thing as good as new.

'Can't have the military operating against anything shabby,' grunted the General. 'Must get it all neat and polished up before we destroy it.'

At last the memorial was sufficiently spick and span to be knocked down. The artillery drew up with their best guns. The streets of Pagwell were cleared. The shops were shut, the children sent to stay with their aunts.

'Mind you make a better job of it than you did with the fountain,' said the General.

A very small, bristly Artillery Major drew himself up to his full height, which put rather a strain on his braces, and shouted in a voice that broke three of the railway station windows.

'Numbah one gun fiyah!'

*Boom!* Number one gun fired. When the smoke had cleared away the memorial was still there, but parts of it were a bit dirty and had to be washed again.

'Numbah two gun fiyah!' yelled the Major.

*Boom!* all over again.

The Major's voice chipped a bit of concrete lace off the canopy, but the shell bounced off the statue's waistcoat and blew a hole in the road.

All that day the Artillery Major screamed, 'Numbah something gun fiyah!' The guns boomed and banged. Clouds of smoke went up and came down again but the memorial only took on a slightly more sinister sneer.

'All guns fiyah!' screeched the Major.

*Boom! Bang! Bonketty boom!*

One of the shells missed the memorial entirely and shot a little turret off the station, which dropped on the top of the memorial and made it even bigger than before.

But still not a single chip fell off the memorial.

'Fetch Professor Branestawm!' cried the Mayor, tearing his hair and wishing the memorial could be torn apart as easily. 'He invented the thing. Let him demolish it.'

'Er, um, ah,' said the Professor. 'You must remem-

'*Do you mean the thing is there for ever?*' gasped
the Mayor

ber,' he said, 'that I invented a special material for this memorial, one that would withstand the rigours of the weather, need no maintenance and never decay.'

'Do you mean the thing is there for ever?' gasped the Mayor.

'When I was asked to devise this memorial,' said the Professor, 'I understood that it was to be in lasting memory of the first Lord, um, ah, Pagwell. If I had been told it was to be a temporary memorial, a momentary monument, so to speak, I should have acted differently. However, since you wish this memorial demolished I will see what I can do.'

He went into his inventory to invent a memorial-demolishing machine. The first machine nearly demolished the inventory, the second one demolished the Professor's dinner and the third one demolished itself.

'Er, um,' said the Professor, putting custard into his coffee in mistake for milk and thinking it tasted rather better. 'Possibly a new kind of explosive with devastating but limited effect.'

To begin with that wasn't any good because nobody could make a hole in the monument to put the explosive in.

Then the Professor inserted some of the explosive into a gap between the mermaids and Lord Pagwell's throne. Everyone retired immediately, as if it were firework night, and the Professor set off the charge.

*Bam, krarrsh!* The explosive went off in a cloud

of striped smoke. All the birds in Great Pagwell rose straight up in the air and then came down again. One of the mermaids now had an orange beard with blue spots but otherwise the memorial was unchanged.

Deadlock had been reached. There was Great Pagwell stuck with an immovable object in the shape of the Lord Pagwell Memorial, but where was the irresistible force to try to move it with?

That night there was the thunderstorm of the century.

'Ha!' said everyone, which sounded very strange if you happened to be listening. 'Now the memorial will be struck by lightning.'

And it was. The lightning struck it three times, then gave up and went away to strike something easier. The memorial remained unchanged but a mermaid's head was slightly scorched.

Then two days later, without any warning the indestructible memorial collapsed in a heap of coloured rubble.

'I can't understand it,' said the Professor, shaking his head. 'I can only conclude that the cumulative effect of pneumatic drills, high explosives, artillery fire, pickaxes and lightning must have set up some kind of secondary reaction within the molecules of the material, thus causing delayed disintegration.'

Pagwell Council hadn't the least idea what he was talking about. But if they didn't understand why the memorial had demolished itself, they weren't going to argue, in case it reconstituted itself when they weren't looking. In no time at all men in funny hats carried the memorial away in wheelbarrows, swept the place clean and left the station yard clear for cars to park illegally.

'Now,' said the Mayor, at the next Council meeting. 'What shall we have in place of the memorial? We can't leave the space empty, it looks so vacant.'

'Arrh,' said one of the Councillors, who always looked a bit vacant himself. 'How about a nice fountain?'

'We've already got a fountain,' said the Town Clerk, 'as you can see if you look out of the window.'

Another Councillor said it would be a good idea to have a hospital as the new memorial since that would be more useful. But there were already a great many hospitals in the Pagwells and not enough nurses to go round.

'I suggest a clock tower,' said the Town Clerk, who always forgot to wind up his watch and depended on public clocks to run his private life.

'Yes, that might encourage the trains to run to time,' said a Councillor, who managed to catch a train only by arriving at the station just too late to catch the previous one.

'But the old memorial had a clock on it,' protested another Councillor. 'We don't want all that trouble over again.'

'Nonsense,' cried the Mayor. 'It wasn't the clock that caused the trouble, it was the rest of it. Anyway we needn't have an elaborate clock that plays tunes and all that stuff. Just a nice, quiet, chiming clock.'

So Professor Branestawm was asked to invent a clock tower with a nice, quiet, chiming clock on it to go where the awful memorial used to be.

'No mermaids, mind,' said the Mayor. 'No fancy work, no outlandish ideas. And for goodness sake make sure it doesn't obstruct the traffic. We don't want cars running into it as they did the memorial.'

'Um, ah, er, yes,' said the Professor, mentally crossing out all the outlandish ideas he was having.

He went into his inventory and started inventing like mad. 'They shall have their nice, quiet clock tower,' he muttered. 'I won't give them any outlandish ideas. They're going to have the plainest, most ordinary, dull, unimaginative, miserable clock tower that ever was.'

They certainly did. The clock tower was dark black all over and chimed in a whisper. It stood on legs so that people could drive cars under it. It had no mermaids, no floral wreaths, not even a fancy scroll.

But there's no pleasing some people, as they say. Letters began to pour in from the residents of Great Pagwell, complaining that the new clock tower was too quiet, too plain, too uninteresting and too nearly everything they thought it ought not to be.

Some people wanted the clock to show metric time because of the Common Market. Others *didn't* want it to be metric in case it meant they only had ten hours in a day instead of twelve. Some people said couldn't the clock tower be arranged to sell soft drinks and hard ice-creams for people waiting for trains. Others wanted it to have illuminated maps of Great Pagwell on it so that people could find their way about. Still others thought it would be nice to have a dovecote on top so that pigeons could fly in and out and make it look like a cuckoo clock tower.

One or two people wanted it to show news films. Mr Pryce-Rize would have liked it to broadcast news of the latest bargains at his supermarket. The Vicar was all for having the times of services posted on it and thought he might even conduct special clock tower services in it. Colonel Dedshott felt it would be a good saluting base for military parades and the Head Policeman said it ought to broadcast traffic instructions and dire warnings against parking cars anywhere at any time.

'Pah!' snorted Professor Branestawn. He threw all the letters up in the air. 'Serve them right for having my other memorial destroyed. If they don't like it they can lump it.'

But lumping clock towers, especially Professor Branestawm clock towers, takes a bit of doing. Complaining is easier.

The situation was awful. But then, on the fifth morning after the clock tower was finished, it fell down half-way through striking eight and everyone near enough to hear it thought it was only four o'clock and went to sleep again. They would have been late for work but fortunately it was Sunday.

'You, um, ah, see what comes of trying to tell me what sort of clock tower to invent,' said the Professor to the Town Clerk, while the collapsed tower was being carted away. 'Now perhaps you will kindly let me, ah, um, know best.'

The next clock tower was the sort of thing you dream about when you've had too much supper. It had an illuminated clock that chimed and struck as often as possible and played tunes in between. It had ornamental balconies and fancy spires and exotic minarets. It gave out weather forecasts, it explained how to get to almost anywhere, it gave warning of the approach of trains and it sold you chocolate, lemonade-flavoured crisps and coconut-flavoured peanuts, if you put the right coins in the right slots and moved out of the way quickly enough to avoid getting the goods in your eye.

It was certainly the clock tower of all clock towers.

But it didn't have any mauve mermaids.

'I think I may, um, ah, say without fear of, ah, contradiction,' said the Professor, 'that this time the Council will have nothing to complain of.'

But the new clock tower kept the sun out of the Station-master's sitting-room just as effectively as the old memorial had done. People still ran into it in their cars. Others tried to buy special cheap-rate tickets at it. Passengers still thought it was a waiting-room and wrote rude letters of complaint when they found it wasn't, and Lady Pagwell continued to scrape expensive bits off her car on it.

But it didn't have any mauve mermaids which was something.

## II

# *The Wandering Wedding Present*

*Rat-a-tat* came a knock at Professor Branestawm's front door. It was the postman, with an enormous envelope too big to go in the letter-box. The Professor opened it and took out a card almost as enormous, with wiggly gilt edges.

'Ha!' said the Professor. 'Secret message. But who from? And what sort of, ah, message would it be when the card is completely blank?'

Mrs Flittersnoop put down her duster and turned the card over so that the Professor could read the printed side.

'Why, it's an invitation to a wedding,' she cried, reading it herself.

'I can't possibly go,' said the Professor. 'I am lecturing somewhere.'

'Oh, but you must,' said Mrs Flittersnoop, who would rather have gone to a wedding once than the pictures ten times, because she got a better cry.

But the Professor wasn't keen on weddings, partly because getting dressed for a wedding with all the right clothes on the right way round was quite beyond him and partly because he could never be sure of arriving at the right place and usually turned up at a museum or library or college, none of which are really popular places for people to get married in.

'I'm sure I'm lecturing somewhere on that day,' he said, 'or if I'm not I shall have to, er, arrange to be. When is it?' he asked.

Mrs Flittersnoop told him. 'It's Lord and Lady Pagwell's daughter, the Hon. Priscilla Pagwell,' she said. 'She's getting married to Captain Jinglespurs of the Heavy Hussars. The ceremony is to be at the village church of Snorting-Busby because his parents live there but the reception is to be at Parva Towers because Lord and Lady Pagwell live *there*.'

'It's a long way from Snorting-Busby to Parva Towers, which if I, ah, remember is at Pagwell Parva,' said the Professor, who often knew where places were although he could hardly ever manage to get to them.

'Yes indeed, I'm sure, sir,' said Mrs Flittersnoop, passing a careful hand over the wedding invitation in case it had got dusty. 'But I believe these society people have to arrange it like that, so that the bride and bridegroom can rush off to the reception place and be ready to greet their guests looking as if they'd been there all the time.'

'It sounds most, er, complicated,' said the Professor, shaking his head slowly so that his spectacles slid from side to side. 'Something is sure to go wrong. I find it always does if one has things too, ah, complicated.'

'Well, if you can't go, sir,' said Mrs Flittersnoop, thinking it would be just as well if he didn't, because it would take all the Catapult Cavaliers and most of the Pagwell police force to find the Professor once he got himself really well lost on the way to Snorting-Busby. 'If you can't go, you must send a present anyway.'

'Sending a present anyway is no way to do it,' said the Professor. 'It might get lost or damaged or finish up in the dead letter office.'

'I mean, whether you go or not, you must send a present,' said Mrs Flittersnoop, putting the invitation behind the dining-room clock where it dislodged three bills, a demand for somebody else's water rate and a circular advertising Miss Frenzie's *Slapdash Cook Book for People in a Hurry*.

Just then Miss Frenzie of the Pagwell Publishing Company arrived in person on the back of a bicycle with her secretary Violet almost in the driving-seat.

'Ah, Professor, just the man I want to see,' she exclaimed, jumping off while Violet parked the bicycle against a climbing rose which immediately stopped climbing and fell over. 'Did you receive your invitation to the Hon. Priscilla's wedding?' The Pagwell Publishing Company was owned by Lord Pagwell, and so Miss Frenzie was involved in the wedding preparations and was already planning to write a new book called *Weddings Made Easy* or *How to get your daughter off the shelf without tearing the wallpaper*.

'There's been a bit of a mix-up in the office,' she said, 'and some of the guests have received bills for specially-autographed copies of my *Slapdash Cook Book* by mistake.'

'Er, um, no, yes,' said the Professor, beginning to

*Miss Frenzie of the Pagwell Publishing Company
arrived in person*

wish he wasn't just the man Miss Frenzie wanted to see, as she whisked him into his study and started advising him about what sort of present to send.

'Now you must be original,' she said. 'They'll expect an unusual present from Professor Branestawm. But not one of your inventions,' she added hastily, as she thought she noticed a look of inventing come into the Professor's eyes but it may have been only a reflection from his spectacles. 'I think you should send them a toast rack,' she said.

'A toast rack!' exclaimed the Professor, in as much astonishment as if she had suggested his sending a Chinese bicycle stand. 'But that is hardly, um, er, original, Miss Frenzie. I have no doubt a good many people will send toast racks.'

'That's just it,' said Miss Frenzie, waving his papers about, 'everybody will think that, so nobody will send a toast rack. You, with your brilliant intelligence and knowledge of the human mind, will send a present that dares to be so ordinary that it will be exquisitely original.'

'Hm,' said the Professor. But he knew better than to argue with Miss Frenzie and anyway he had no chance to because she swept him off to the silverware department of Ginnibag & Knitwoddle's and had him immersed in silver toast racks.

'Well, I do think that's nice, I'm sure, sir,' said Mrs Flittersnoop, when the Professor brought home the toast rack. 'There's nothing like a nice silver toast rack for a wedding present, I always say.'

'I, er, hope they like toast,' murmured the Professor.

'Oh well, it doesn't matter, I'm sure, sir,' said Mrs Flittersnoop. 'A magnificent large toast rack like this they could always use for storing LP records, or putting letters in ready for the post. I'll just go and pack it up nicely for you to send off.'

She bustled away and the Professor went off into dreams of inventing a non-noisy explosive which General Shatterfortz would absolutely love as it would give him a chance to blow up the enemy before they knew it had happened.

Meantime Mrs Flittersnoop had found a nice clean shoe-box, packed the toast rack in plenty of tissue paper, wrapped the box neatly in brown paper and put it ready for the Professor to take to the post, being careful to leave a note beside it of the address of the Hon. Priscilla as she was sure the Professor wouldn't have known it or would have forgotten it if he had.

'Well, thank you very much, Mrs Flittersnoop,' said the Professor, coming reluctantly away from non-noisy explosives and putting his hat on the right way round by mistake. And off he went to post the magnificent toast rack.

When he got back Mrs Flittersnoop was in all the dithers she could manage, which was a great many.

'Oh, my goodness gracious me, I'm sure, sir!' she cried, waving her hands. 'You took the wrong parcel, sir. That wasn't the toast rack you took, it was a pair of my old shoes I'd parcelled up to take round to the repairers. Oh dear, dear, whatever will the Hon. Priscilla think when she gets a pair of old shoes for a wedding present?'

'I always thought,' said the Professor, 'that people liked old shoes at weddings. They tie them on places, so I understand.' Miss Frenzie's flattering remarks about his brilliant intelligence and knowledge of the human mind had gone to his head a bit.

'Yes, yes, of course, old shoes tied on the wedding car are very nice and traditional,' said Mrs Flitter-snoop, 'but not for a wedding present. They'll look awful on the long table at Parva Towers, among all the silver things other people will have sent. You must go to the post office, sir, and get the parcel back.'

But the post office men were most reluctant to give the Professor any parcels. Once they had got their hands on something they weren't going to let it go until they had safely delivered it.

'Er, um, this is most awkward,' said the Professor, and he went along to Colonel Dedshott to see if he could get him to send a detachment of Catapult Cavaliers to detach the parcel from the post office.

'Ha, Branestawm, glad to see you, my word, what!' cried the Colonel. 'When you were here earlier on you left a parcel behind.'

'Oh, ah, really?' exclaimed the Professor. 'I'm so glad.'

'You mean to say you're glad you left a parcel behind!' said the Colonel, wondering if the Professor's inventing mind was going a bit wobbly. 'But didn't you mean to post it? It had stamps on it and everything, y'know, by Jove!'

'Er, um, ah, yes, I did intend to post it,' said the Professor, 'in fact, I was afraid I *had* posted it.'

The Colonel's head began to go round ever so slowly, as it usually did rather quickly when the Professor explained his inventions.

'Why were you afraid you'd posted it if you meant to post it, confound it?' he cried, so loudly that his two Catapult Cavalier butlers shot in and stood to attention, expecting to get a frightful military ticking off for something; they didn't know what, but then soldiers are never quite sure what they are being ordered about for, what with doing it all by numbers and military stuff like that.

'Ha, there you are!' said the Colonel, not stopping to think where else they could be. 'Professor Branestawm left a parcel here. Meant to post it. Know where it is?'

'Yes, sir,' said the two Catapult Cavalier butlers together. 'We assumed the article was intended for the post, sir, so we posted it, sir.' They clicked their heels, saluted and went out.

'This is terrible,' groaned the Professor, sinking into a chair, but not sinking very far as it was a hard and military wooden one.

'What's terrible about finding a parcel you forgot to post has been posted for you?' asked the Colonel, his head starting to go round a bit faster the more he didn't understand things.

'It's the wrong parcel,' cried the Professor, flinging his arms wide and knocking down a coloured photo of General Shatterfortz. 'It's a wedding present for Lord Pagwell's daughter.'

'What do you mean, it's the wrong parcel,' said Colonel Dedshott. 'If it's a present for Lord Pagwell's daughter, why didn't you want it posted?'

'Because it is actually a, er, pair of Mrs Flittersnoop's old shoes,' cried the Professor. 'I picked up the wrong parcel. I should have taken the one with the toast rack in it. Good gracious!' He suddenly clapped his hands to his head and disarranged his spectacles. 'If I have sent Mrs Flittersnoop's old shoes to Lord Pagwell's daughter, that means Mrs Flittersnoop will have taken the silver toast rack to the shoe repairers to be soled and heeled.'

Colonel Dedshott tried to visualize a silver toast rack being soled and heeled. Then his military mind saw a solution to the problem.

'Send a telegram to the Hon. Priscilla,' he cried. 'Do not open parcel from Branestawm stop mistake stop correct parcel coming stop.'

But Professor Branestawm thought another visit to the post office would only complicate things more. So he went along to the shoe repairers to see if getting a silver toast rack back from them was easier than getting old shoes back from the post office.

'What's that?' asked the Head Shoe Repairer, looking at the Professor over his spectacles, while the Professor looked back at him over and under several pairs of his own. 'A silver toast rack, did you say? We don't repair those, you know. Not our trade. Dear me, no. If it had been a leather toast rack, now, we might have managed that. But no toast racks have been brought in, have they, Joe?' he called.

'No, I haven't seen one,' said Joe's voice from inside a noisy little room at the back.

'Sorry, sir,' said the Head Shoe Repairer. 'Hasn't been brought here. Try the jewellers.'

So Professor Branestawm went home, to be met by Mrs Flittersnoop in a frightful state, her hair waving about nearly as much as Miss Frenzie's. 'Haven't you got it back, sir?' she cried. 'Oh, dearie me! I don't know what Lady Pagwell will say, I'm sure, sir. We shall just have to send off the silver toast rack and hope they won't notice the old shoes very much.'

'You mean you didn't, ah, take the silver toast rack to the shoe repairers, after all?' gasped the Professor.

'No, indeed, sir!' said Mrs Flittersnoop. 'I've got it here safe and sound.'

Of course the Professor should have known that Mrs Flittersnoop wasn't likely to take a silver toast rack to the shoe repairers.

'Well, um, ah, that's something,' he said. 'We must just send off the silver toast rack and hope for the best.'

So Mrs Flittersnoop carefully posted the silver toast rack and came back and made a nice strong cup of tea which she felt they could both do with.

The wedding reception for the Hon. Priscilla and

Captain Jinglespurs was raging happily. The wedding presents were tastefully displayed on the billiard table, previously covered with a lace cloth belonging to Lady Pagwell's great-grandmother. And among the presents stood the magnificent Branestawm toast rack with a polite note in Mrs Flittersnoop's handwriting.

But, thank goodness Mrs Flittersnoop's old shoes were nowhere to be seen! The Professor had been so immersed in his non-noisy explosive he had addressed the parcel to himself instead of to the Hon. Priscilla. So the old shoes were lucky for weddings after all because they went straight back to Mrs Flittersnoop.

And the whole wedding went off fine, except for a bit of bother over the photographs, because the Hon. Priscilla didn't like having her photograph taken. The pictures always made her look like a severe school teacher instead of the glamorous society beauty she liked to think of herself as.

And Captain Jinglespurs persuaded Professor Branestawm to invent him a special, high velocity, pop-up toaster which shot the toast up in the air. Then he fired at it with an airgun to keep in practice for clay pigeon shooting. The Hon. Priscilla said she didn't mind really although it did make rather a lot of holes in the dining-room ceiling when he missed and rather a lot of crumbs on the carpet when he didn't.

# The Branestawm Bank Robbery

ONE Thursday morning, Professor Branestawm had lost all five pairs of his spectacles and was trying to tune in to a talk on the washing machine, thinking it was the radio, when a large and slightly shabby car drew up outside and out of it got two men with pale faces and dark glasses.

'We're from Pagwell University,' said one, who was wearing a raincoat. 'Professor Branestawm is giving a lecture this afternoon and we've come to fetch him.'

'To save him the trouble of getting lost,' said the other man, who had a beard and very large ears.

'You didn't say you were lecturing at Pagwell University, sir,' said Mrs Flittersnoop, when she had found the Professor after looking in several places where he wasn't and bumping into him where she didn't know he was.

'I, er, um, am I?' said the Professor. 'I, er, must have forgotten to tell you or else I forgot I was going to, that is to say, I mean, I must have forgotten that I was going to tell you that I was going to lecture to . . .'

'Come along, Professor,' said the man in the raincoat. 'We must be getting along or you'll be late and you wouldn't like that, now, would you?'

'Er yes, of course,' said the Professor, meaning, no, he wouldn't like to be late. They all got into the car which rolled off, leaving Mrs Flittersnoop wondering what to do with the chop she had got for the Professor's lunch and deciding to have it for her own dinner, if the Professor wasn't back by then.

'It's very kind of you to come and fetch me,' said the Professor to the two pale-faced, dark-glasses men in the car. 'As a matter of fact, the last time I went to the University I didn't get there as I had some difficulty with the railway.'

'Yes. Railways is easy things to have difficulty with,' said Beard and Ears.

'Quite,' said the Professor, thinking people from Universities ought to talk better grammar than that but thinking perhaps they were from the window-cleaning department of the University, or worked there at sweeping garden paths, where you didn't need the same sort of careful grammar you have to have if you're in the gown-and-lecture division.

Presently the car drew up at a house that looked as if one of the Professor's inventions had been at it. The two men got out.

'I, er, am afraid you have lost the way,' said the Professor. 'It's a thing I often do myself.'

Raincoat opened the door of what was left of the house while Beard and Ears pushed the Professor inside. They shut the door, took the Professor into a room furnished with two boxes and a jug of water and locked the door behind them.

'This here's a kidnap,' said Raincoat, not bothering to talk politely any more.

' 'Sright!' said Beard and Ears. 'You're going to invent a machine for us to rob the Pagwell Bank.'

Mrs Flittersnoop finished the chop that should have been for Professor Branestawm's lunch. She watched her favourite programme on the telly. She tidied up the sitting-room for the third time that day, which was a bit unnecessary as the Professor wasn't there to untidy it but Mrs Flittersnoop was always rather anxious about leaving a room to itself in case it got itself disarranged while she wasn't looking.

'The Professor is very late,' she said to herself, looking at the sitting-room clock and counting backwards and forwards to arrive at the time it actually was. 'I do hope he hasn't lost the way. Oh, but then the gentlemen who fetched him will be bringing him back, of course.'

But the gentlemen who had fetched him were at that moment saying extremely impolite things to him while he was trying to make it clear to them that he wasn't going to invent a bank-robbing machine for them.

Mrs Flittersnoop telephoned Pagwell University to ask if the Professor was there and they said he wasn't, which was quite true. They didn't think it was necessary to say that he hadn't been there that day because Mrs Flittersnoop hadn't thought it necessary to ask them, as she thought she knew that he had.

'Well, I suppose he'll be back soon,' she said. But,

of course, he wasn't back soon, nor later on nor even much, much later on.

'Perhaps the gentlemen with the car have had a breakdown,' she thought.

But when the Professor didn't come home all night, Mrs Flittersnoop rang up the police. But although they had a department for dealing with lost dogs, if the lost dogs came to the police station, or for looking after luggage if someone brought it there, they weren't exactly organized for looking for lost Professors, especially ones like Professor Branestawm, who were absolutely expert at getting lost.

The kidnappers had put the Professor into an upstairs room with quantities of tools and bits of wire and wood and metal and cogwheels and everything else he might need to invent a bank-robbing machine.

'You just invent us that machine and we'll take you home,' they said, bringing him a cup of coffee.

The Professor had no intention of inventing anything so drastic as a bank-robbing machine, but he thought a bit of crafty talk wouldn't be out of place.

'Ah, yes,' he said, clashing his spectacles, which he had fortunately found in various pockets. 'Now if money was attracted by a magnet in the same way as steel washers are, for instance,' he said, 'I could mount a powerful electro-magnet in your van and you would only have to switch it on as you drove past the bank and all the money would come rushing out to you.'

'Great!' shouted the kidnappers. 'You do that.'

'But!' said the Professor, wagging a finger. 'Money is not attracted to magnets so that will not, um, ah, work!'

'Grrr!' growled Raincoat and Beard and Ears, getting fierce. 'We don't want to know what won't work, we want something that does.'

'Then again,' went on the Professor, taking no notice, 'if I could invent a magnet that would attract money, the idea would work perfectly.'

'Great!' they shouted. 'You do that!' and they went out, locking the door.

'Now,' said the Professor to himself, 'all I have to do is to invent a bank-robbing machine for them that won't work although they will think it does. Then they will be foiled, the bank will be safe and the money will stay where it is.'

But he found inventing something that was meant to go wrong wasn't the same thing at all as inventing something that went wrong of its own accord when it wasn't supposed to. He found, too, that trying to invent in the upstairs room of a half-ruined house was a bit difficult. Perhaps he missed not drinking the cups of tea and cocoa Mrs Flittersnoop brought him. He tried not drinking the cup of coffee the kidnappers had brought but that didn't help.

He thought of a thing with long telescopic arms that would shoot in through the bank windows, grab the money and shoot out again. But then he remembered that banks keep money in drawers and safes so that wasn't any good.

He invented an imitation person, hollow inside, that would go into the bank and present a cheque made out for a million pounds. Then while the bank people were looking to see if they had all that money, the imitation person would open, sweep the money in and dash out to the robbers' van.

'Ah, but then I should have to make it go wrong so that the imitation person got caught and the police might recognize my work and arrest me. Oh dear!' The Professor shook his head. 'That's another thing. If I invent a bank-robbing machine, even if it goes wrong, I could be arrested for trying to rob the bank and sent to prison and they don't have inventories in prison so I'd have nothing to do. Perhaps I ought to speak to the prison people about having inventories in prisons . . .'

Just then the Professor heard a familiar sound outside. It was the *clop, clop* of horses' hoofs and the jingle of harness.

'Dedshott!' he cried. He dashed to the window. 'Hurray!' Colonel Dedshott was riding past at the head of a detachment of Catapult Cavaliers.

'Rescue!' shouted the Professor. 'Help! Help! I am kidnapped. Rescue!' He waved his arms but the window was shut and screwed up so no sound got out. Colonel Dedshott, keeping a wary eye out for possible enemies, saw the Professor at the window. He thought the Professor was just waving to him.

'Ha! Branestawm been at his inventing game again,' he grunted. 'Messed up that house, all right. Glad it isn't mine, by Jove!' Then, reckoning he ought to acknowledge the Professor's waves, he saluted and ordered the Catapult Cavaliers to 'Eyes right!' Then they all went clopping and jingling on, leaving the Professor un-rescued.

Mrs Flittersnoop was on the phone to Pagwell University again.

'We haven't seen the Professor for more than a week,' they said.

'But he came to give a lecture yesterday,' said Mrs Flittersnoop.

'No lecture was scheduled for yesterday,' said the University and rang off.

Mrs Flittersnoop, who wasn't quite sure what scheduled meant, didn't see how it could explain the Professor not being there.

'Oh dear, oh dear, whatever has happened to him?' she cried. 'I must ring Colonel Dedshott.'

In the kidnappers' upstairs room the Professor was demonstrating his bank-robbing machine to Raincoat and Beard and Ears.

'Great!' shouted Raincoat, when he saw it work.

'All you have to, er, do,' said the Professor, 'is to push it into the bank. Everyone will think it is a baby in a pram because that is what I have made it look like, as you see.'

'Great!' said Raincoat again. He was a bit short of words.

'But,' went on the Professor, 'it would look rather unusual for two men to be pushing a pram so one of you must dress up as a woman.'

'You'll have to do that,' said Beard and Ears, 'because of my beard.'

'Then you'll pull this lever,' said the Professor.

'And Bob's your uncle!' said Beard and Ears.

The Professor wondered what the kidnappers' relations had to do with robbing banks, but Raincoat and Beard and Ears dashed off with the bank-robbing pram, leaving the professor shut up tight in the room.

'I only hope it goes wrong the right way,' murmured the Professor. 'Now I must get in touch with the police.'

He found he had forgotten the number of Pagwell Police Station, remembered he had it written on a piece of paper but discovered he didn't have the piece of paper with him. Then he found a telephone directory and looked up the number. After that he found there wasn't a telephone.

'I must get out,' he cried, and, grabbing tools from among the things the kidnappers had given him for inventing the bank-robbing machine, he started to pick the lock.

'Tut, tut,' he said, after picking away for a long time. 'I don't understand it. This is an ordinary, cheap lock and I've often opened them when I've lost a key. Oh dear.'

He leant wearily against the door.

It opened.

The kidnappers had forgotten to lock it in their hurry to get disguised and rob the bank. The Professor had been trying to open a locked lock so of course he completely failed to open an unlocked

*Everyone will think it is a baby in a pram because that
is what I have made it look like*

lock. And the door opened outwards instead of inwards because the house was a bit busted up and patched up.

But the Professor was free. He dashed downstairs and saw a bicycle leaning against the wall. He grabbed it and it fell to bits.

'Dear, dear!' he panted. He hauled it upstairs, mended it, dragged it down again, got on and rode up the road. Ten yards later it fell to bits again.

'I must thumb a lift,' cried the Professor.

He held his spectacles on with one hand and waved his other hand. There was nothing coming. Oh yes, there was, though. Good gracious, it was a panda car and it pandered to the Professor enough to pick him up and take him to Pagwell Police Station.

'Now, let's have some details,' said the Chief Policeman, after he had been on the telephone and got quantities of policemen carefully concealed all round the Great Pagwell Bank, up trees and behind fences and inside letter-boxes and anywhere they could leap out and arrest bank robbers on the word of command.

'They're going to bring a pram with a baby in it to the bank,' said the Professor. 'One of them will be disguised as a lady. But, um, ah, the pram does not contain a baby, it contains an invention of mine for robbing banks. That is, my invention will not rob the bank but the robbers think it will. Instead, when they pull the, ah, lever, things will fly out and, er, encircle them. At the same time the machine will emit a loud noise . . .'

'And that will be the signal for my men to dash in and arrest them,' said the Chief Policeman. 'Excellent, Professor. What time is the robbery due?' he asked, rather as if he were inquiring the time of the next bus to somewhere.

'I, ah, really don't know,' said the Professor. 'I fear my watch has stopped.' He shook it and the watch struck fifteen and put out a little sign saying it was Christmas Day, because it was another of the Professor's inventions.

Great Pagwell Bank was busier than busy. Everybody in Great Pagwell seemed to be paying in all the money they had and drawing it all out again. Money was jingling, bank notes were being slapped about. There were cries of, 'How would you like it?' and 'Please sign your usual signature here.' This took one gentleman by surprise because the only signature he knew how to write was a rather unusual one since his name was Hecklethwaite Binglekoster.

In the middle of all this banking business, in walked a lady with a pram and the baby in it decided to throw out a teaset his mum had just bought because he thought it would make a lovely noise. It did. And of course all the hidden policemen thought it was the Professor's bank-robbing machine catching the robbers.

They dashed in with whistles blowing and

truncheons waving. But before they could get the lady and her baby wrongfully arrested, in came men with stockings over their heads and guns in their hands.

'Good gracious!' cried the Professor. 'These aren't my bank robbers either.'

'This is a stick-up,' cried the men, but the stockings over their heads made it sound like, 'Mum wuff glub glub pwouff.'

'Oh no, it isn't,' yelled the policemen, guessing what the robbers had said, and they set about them.

Two lady cashiers fainted into the banknotes and a gentleman cashier threw a bag of 1p pieces at the robbers. The bag split and the coins rolled all over the floor. Robbers and policemen and bank customers scrambled for them. One of the robbers fired his gun just as Professor Branestawm's bank robbers came in with their pram. The bullet hit the Professor's bank-robbing machine, which instantly made frightful noises and produced yards of twisty barbed wire which snarled up everyone in the bank, including the policemen.

Then in dashed Colonel Dedshott and a detachment of Catapult Cavaliers who had promised Mrs Flittersnoop to look for the Professor. They were followed by Commander Hardaport (Retired) and some sailors, and after them came Dr Mumpzanmeazle and a dozen nurses in case anyone needed bandaging.

Pandemonium reigned. It did more, it hailed and thundered. Booklets telling you how the bank can

help you flew about without helping anyone. The
baby in the pram put on a policeman's helmet and
threw out an extra jug he had overlooked. The
policemen ran out of handcuffs, but the nurses tied
up the robbers even more effectively with bandages,
while Dr Mumpzanmeazle rushed round giving the
robbers injections that sent them to sleep at once,
and they dreamt the police were helping them to
rob the Bank of England but all the bank had in
stock were stale chocolate coins and last year's meat
pies.

'I'm extremely obliged to you, Professor,' said the
Bank Manager, who had made up his mind to leave
the bank and join the army because it seemed safer,
but had changed his mind back again when all the
robbers were carted away.

'Er, um, ah, thank you,' said the Professor, and he
drew out a nice big chunk of money to take himself
and Mrs Flittersnoop out to dinner to make up for
everything.